How Not

To

Worry About

The

Love Life

Of

Spiders

HOW NOT TO WORRY ABOUT THE LOVE LIFE OF SPIDERS

EARL TUCKER

Illustrated by

HAROLD E. PRICE

Wildside Press

FOREWORD

Our author Earl Tucker feels that Confucius was something of a big time "POP OFF" in his day, but that Confucius was right when he made his famous statement: "Give the public what it wants."

Whether or not Earl is quoting Confucius exactly word for word, the public did overwhelmingly want his (Earl's, not Confucius') first book, RAMBLING ROSES AND FLYING BRICKS, so much so that right off the book sold out completely. Meanwhile, for every funny story in RAMBLING ROSES AND FLYING BRICKS many people remembered at least twice as many other hilarious Tucker stories, that should have been included. So again, as Confucius may have said: "It was the people, not us, who requested HOW NOT TO WORRY ABOUT THE LOVE LIFE OF SPIDERS, and other selections, by Earl Tucker."

However, we ourselves are right proud to be involved in this, another great work by one of this country's leading humorists, whose genius remains his main claim to fame. Whether or not you read him in print, or hear him lecture, Earl Tucker continues to help people who have trouble worrying about things like spiders.

David Strode Akens

Strike One

Strike Two

Strike Out

I

Are Firing Squads Courteous?

On a recent trip to Florida I was stopped by a highway patrolman. When he asked to see my license, I shut off the motor because I knew it was going to be a long, drawn-out search, on account of my billfold is abundantly filled with practically everything except money.

Somewhere among the papers and cards in my pocketbook was a driver's license, but I wasn't in any particular hurry to find it because I was an hour ahead of schedule and, too, I was just a little lonesome from driving alone.

"This," I said, looking at one of the cards, "is an Alabama hunting license. See, on the back side is pasted a duck stamp. I paid three bucks for the stamp and I ain't seen duck one. Do you people down here have much good duck hunting?"

9

THE LOVE LIFE OF SPIDERS

"All I hunt," the patrolman answered, "is people who don't have a license to drive." He acted a little bit irritated, but I figured he was maybe just tired or something. Too, I felt rather sorry for him. That kind of hunting must get awfully boring, and I'll bet there are some days when he doesn't catch more than two or three.

"Now here," I said, continuing my search through the cards, "is one that shows I'm a member of the Alabama Press Association and here's one that says I'm a member of the Lodge and in good standing. We have a pretty good Lodge in Thomasville, that's where I'm from, although I don't go out to the meetings like I should. A fellow who belongs to an organization sure ought to go to the meetings, don't you think?"

"A fellow ought to have his driver's license where he can get to it, too," this highly dressed up patrolman observed. The way he snapped at me I don't think he belongs to the Lodge.

Cars and trucks were piling up behind us and he was getting pretty impatient, so I gave him a handful of cards to look through, thinking we might speed it up a little.

"That one," I said pointing to a card he had just picked up, "shows I'm a licensed real estate broker in Alabama. It's kind of a sideline with me and my partner, a Mr. Morgan. We don't make much out of it. You know, people who have something to sell think it's worth twice as much as it really is and people who want to buy something think they ought to get it for half what it's worth. You sure can't make much in the real estate business."

Behind us the cars had started blowing and a big truck driver directly behind us was shaking his fist and saying something I'm mighty glad I couldn't make out. I'm too old to fight when people call me names like that. At least half the people behind us probably didn't have any place to go, so I kept searching through the cards.

11

THE LOVE LIFE OF SPIDERS

"This is a card showing I have liability insurance in case I hit somebody or something. I never had to use it, but the satisfaction of knowing I'm protected is worth something. Now that card you have there shows I'm a member of the Auburn Alumni Association. We had a pretty good football team this year. You didn't have much at Florida did you?" He didn't say anything, but maybe he didn't hear me, on account of the racket from 50 or 60 cars behind.

That's when I asked him to come around and sit down in the car, so we could start back through the cards as one of us had undoubtedly missed the driver's license somewhere.

Instead of accepting my invitation, though, he looked at me, and his lips were quivering and his face was getting red, on account of the truck driver, I reckon, and he said, "Buddy, let's just play like you've got a license and forget all about it." He was real nice, I thought. If you'll treat an officer friendly, like I did, you'll find they'll treat you friendly. He'll probably remember me a long time, on account of I was so extra friendly.

12

II

It Is Warmer To Sit On The South Goal Line

It's strange how I always get tickets on the goal line. It's not because I don't order in time. The tickets I got for the Gator Bowl I ordered between halves at the Alabama-Auburn game. I've tried everything. I joined the Alumni Association and that year I got tickets on the north goal line. The next year I got smart and sent my order to Dr. Ralph Draughon, Auburn president who's an old pal of mine. I came out a little better. My tickets were on the south goal line, where it was a trifle warmer and a hundred yards nearer home.

HOW NOT TO WORRY ABOUT

14

THE LOVE LIFE OF SPIDERS

Actually, this is the first year it has mattered much about tickets to the Auburn games. Heretofore so few people came out to see 'em play you could sit most anywhere you pleased, including the players' bench.

The dream of all college athletic directors is to have a stadium where all the seats are on the 50-yard line which would enable them to keep all the old grads happy. A sliding gridiron might solve the problem, but you've got to watch anything that smacks of communism these days. Remember what happened to the story of Robin Hood.

Seats on the goal line, though, aren't as bad as you might think. Theoretically, I should be able to see half the touchdowns that are scored. I would, too, except the quarter ends just before they score. The timekeeper must have a brother on the other goal line.

I've felt for a number of years that I should be given a free ticket to all the games. My presence there adds so much to the pleasure of the spectators. For instance, they use my bald head as a land-mark in pointing out people in the stadium. "There's Johnny Smith—right in front of that bald-headed man," you can hear 'em say. "That's Jimmy Brown—three seats to the right of that bald-headed man." They never say a fellow is six rows down and seven seats from the end and they never use a fat man or a lady with a red hat in locating people. It's always me. My bald head is the aiming point for everybody in Section Z. Some of these days I'm going to start wearing a hat and there'll be a lot of people crossed up.

Should you ever need to find me at a football game, pick out the most boisterous drunk in the stands and I'll be next to him. If there's only one among the 40,000 fans he's always nearest me. On my other side will be a little boy who spends the afternoon climbing over me for his frequent trips to the men's room.

HOW NOT TO WORRY ABOUT

Too, I don't know how the fans in the center of the aisle would get along without me. I'm the middle man in the soft-drink and hot dog business. I pass the wares of the peddlers back and forth and help them with their change.

If you still can't find me, just look for the bald-headed man. There's a three-headed man right behind me and a gentleman wearing a coon-skin cap with a pink feather in it is seated in front of me. They arn't conspicuous, though.

Just look for the bald-headed man. That's me.

III

Is A Two-Headed Man Prominent?

It's bad to be kind of dumb, like I am. A couple of fast-talking fellows came in the office recently and said they were contacting just a few of the prominent citizens, and that I had been selected as one to receive a brand-new set of encyclopedias as part of a nation-wide introductory campaign. From what they said I figured they wanted me to have the set free so they could tell everybody I had 'em and it might help their company to sell a flock of the things around town. I was highly flattered and mighty glad to accommodate the two men who seemed like mighty fine, intelligent fellows. The way the thing turned out, though, the books weren't free at all and before they left I had to plank down $9.95 as down payment. I just didn't have the heart to tell the men that I really wasn't so prominent.

There's another fellow who comes around once a year selling subscriptions to a farm magazine. On account of me being
so prominent, he always comes to see me first and in addition to
getting the magazine a whole year I get a map of the United
States and its possessions, an extra large map of Alabama
showing its rivers, streams and mountains and a picture of all
the Presidents of the United States. On the back is a table showing the number of pints in a gallon, and so on and the population of all of our principal cities. It's a good deal, although I
never have time to read the magazine and don't need the map
because I already know the way to Hal's Lake. I already know
how many pints in a gallon and as far as I'm concerned George
Washington was the last President who wasn't a politician. On
account of being prominent like I am, though, I feel like I should
continue taking the magazine. While he claims he only calls on
the outstanding citizens in each town, I did notice that after
he left my office he started talking to a Mississippi truck driver
with a load of watermelons and roasting ears.

Political aspirants come around to see me about 6 months
before an election and tell me they're out talking to a few
"influential citizens" in each town to find out whether they
should run or not. In a case like this, always tell 'em to run.
They're going to run anyway. Don't ever let 'em know you're
not influential, either, because they might get elected and there's
no telling when you'll have a cousin or somebody in jail you
want to get out.

Another time it's bad to be prominent is when people need
letters of recommendation. In the last thirty years I must have
written a thousand. The applicant, in my letters, always "comes
from a splendid Christian family" and is invariably "honest,
industrious with a fine personality." The lying I have done! Some
of the folks I have written letters for and bragged on would
rob our cash drawer while I'm writing the letter and some of

18

'em are so lazy they wouldn't get out of a rocking chair to kill a snake. Of course, many of the people I write letters for are very deserving and everything I say they are. The reason I write the same letter for all is because I want to help the deserving ones and others I want to get out of town.

In many other ways, though, I'm not so prominent. I'm powerfully un-prominent with highway patrolmen, game wardens, automobile finance companies and people who loan money.

However, I'll be glad to write you a letter. Let's see. You come from a splendid Christian family and . . .

IV

Did King Tut Carry Burial Insurance?

$\mathbf{M}$onday was some kind of a "letter day" in my life. I paid out my burial insurance policy. The policy I took out fifteen years ago is all paid up and the company is standing by now, ready to pay off its obligation to me.

Well, I'm not rushing them. In fact, I'm doing everything in my power to save them all that trouble and expense for a long, long time.

There's something kind of sad, though, about paying out my policy. The collector came around every month and collected a dollar from me. Every third month it was a dollar and a quarter. It seemed to me that the insurance company had a calendar that had more weeks per month than mine had, but I didn't fuss much about it when he said it had five weeks. In fact, I was always glad to see him, because it reminded me to turn another page on the calendar. I can say this for the collector: In all the fifteen years I don't think he missed calling the first work day of the month a single time, and I don't believe the time of day ever varied fifteen minutes. He was punctuality personified.

People used to be superstitious about burial insurance. They said it was just like buying a casket, putting it under the bed, and waiting for the Death Angel to descend. Well, it's not like that at all. When you buy a casket and put it under the bed you have a lot of money tied up in something you might not need for years to come. Of course, it's a nice place to store blankets and winter clothes, but some people are funny about utilizing the space. When you take out a burial policy you pay for your casket in convenient monthly or weekly payments, if there is anything convenient about paying out money, especially for something you don't want to ever have delivered.

I've always had a sneaking suspicion that burial policy men know as much about the affairs of the people of a community as the telephone operators. But like operators, they refuse to let us in on any of the local gossip, so it never has helped any. A policy man, who goes to just about every home in town, has one big advantage over the ice man. He doesn't have to worry about a truck load of ice melting.

Monday, when I made the last payment, we had a little celebration here in the office, just my policy man and me. We sent out and got a soft drink and drank a toast to the company that will square everything with the undertaker when the Grim Reaper starts whacking away with that sickle of his.

Burial insurance companies have done a lot of good in this country. Time was when hardly a week passed but what I had to give fifty cents to help somebody get buried. Once, inside of six months, I helped bury the same man three times, but he was such a shiftless skunk that I never did grumble about it. Finally he really died and I gave a dollar. Reckon it was the best dollar I ever spent. Nowadays, though, it seems to me that everybody must have a policy, because I never get called on any more to aid in the putting away of some unfortunate soul.

When I got to thinking about how I was going to miss the calls of the policy man, I was kind of worried, but not for long. He came back and sold me a "vault" policy. It costs 44c a month (55c for five-week months) and they'll put the casket I have already paid for in the vault I've just started paying for. He explained that if I died any time in the next few years the company would lose money on me. Brother, I want that company to get rich!

V

Do Bumble Bees Have Over-Possessive Mothers?

A swarm of bees has moved into the attic of my house. People who have never had a bee-hive right in their own home can't realize how blessed they are.

The bees came last week and started their low, weird humming, which is probably part of their honey-making activities. It appears to me that they could make just as much honey and probably make it better without all that noise-making, but that comes under the heading of their business. The location they picked out for their happy home, though, comes under the heading of my business. One stung me Saturday night, which was bad. Sunday morning one stung my housekeeper, which was worse. She threatens to leave unless something is done about the bee question, and done quick. Says she can get a job just as good at some house that isn't operating a bee business.

The thing has me stumped, because I don't know any more about bees than I do about filling out an income tax form. All my life, bees and I have cooperated beautifully, we having adopted one of those "you go your way and I'll go my way" treaties. They didn't bother me and I didn't molest their honey. Even now, after the stinging incident, I'm still willing for them to leave peacefully, and they can take their honey with them as far as I'm concerned.

Naturally, one turns to his friends when troubles strike, but let me say right now that they are of absolutely no help in trying times such as I now face. They can offer all kinds of ridiculous and impractical methods of getting rid of the bees, but none of them are any help in ousting my unwanted tenants. One friend told me to get an old plow and beat on it with a hammer. I tried this. People passing by saw me out in the yard banging away on a plow and they all gave me that "I've been expecting it" look. That's the kind of look where they shake their heads and appear real sad like. I quit the plow-beating on account of so many people already think I'm crazy. I have to be extra careful about things like that.

One friend told me to get a goat, or preferably, two goats. Said bees just won't stay around a place where goats stayed, which makes me respect the bees a little more. They don't have anything on me.

Another friend (acquaintance type) informed me that maybe the government had some kind of special agency that made a business of issuing pamphlets on how to get rid of bees. He thought maybe they would even send an apiarist down from

Washington to assist me. That's the trouble with the government now—you ask for somebody who knows something about bees and they wind up sending you an apiarist. Besides, I'd just about as soon put up with the bees as a government man.

My neighbor takes an entirely different attitude about my bees. He thinks I should let them remain in the loft. Frankly, I think he's expecting me to send him a bucket of honey when it gets ripe for robbing. Sure hope he has plenty of sweetening around the house he can make out on until I rob a bee-loft.

Probably the most revolting suggestion came from a scholarly friend who suggested that I study the bees. He told how they organized and worked and stored up something for the winter months and all that stuff. I say nuts to all that tripe. The way I see it they work hard and store up more than they need and somebody comes along and takes all of it except enough to keep them going until another season so they can be robbed again. If that's smart I'm a monkey's uncle.

Please do not offer any suggestions about how to get rid of bees. If you want the bees, or know somebody who does want some bees, just go ahead with whatever plan suits you. Leave me out of it.

Sf '29 Was Just A Panic, Let's Try To Avoid Depressions

Lots of people still call that thing we had in 1929 and the early thirties a depression, but I've always figured it was a panic. Young people under 25 don't know anything about it, but I'm telling you it was a bad thing! Big business men were jumping off of tall buildings. Poor people couldn't afford to jump on account of their families didn't have the money for a funeral.

While it was bad, I don't remember hearing of anybody starving to death. I did see one family living in an improvised

THE LOVE LIFE OF SPIDERS

tent and they were boiling a rabbit in a pot in the front yard. They couldn't fry the rabbit, they said, because they didn't have any lard. I remember hearing a man tell how they had dried peas for dinner and supper and for breakfast they made patties out of what was left and fried them in sow-belly grease. Actually, he was bragging about having sow-belly, which lots of people didn't have. This fellow belonged to the upper-class.

It always seemed mighty silly to me to see a person jump off a tall building because he was afraid he was going to lose his fortune. If I'm ever faced with the possibility of losing what little I've accumulated, I'm certainly not going to throw in my life, too. Debt sometimes causes people to commit suicide. I've always figured that if there's any suicide-committing on account of my debts, the fellow I owe can do it. He has more to worry about than I have.

In spite of all the hardships that accompanied the depression, though, one thing stands out in my mind very clearly, and that was the happiness among the people. Folks, who had no idea where their groceries for the next week would come from, actually laughed and joked about their predicament. In-laws moved in and several families would live in the same house and they all seemed to be happy. There was mighty little to argue about because nobody had anything. It's the only time that everybody kept up with the Jones', and the reason for that was the Jones' were busted too.

Children nowadays spend as much in one day on ice cream, soft drinks, gasoline and rockola machines as an entire family spent back then in a week for the bare necessities of life. Of course, children have a heap more fun now, especially at Christmastime. It was mighty hard for a kid to get real jubilant over two pieces of stick-candy, a small apple and a sackful of hickory nuts.

Like I said, nobody got hungry that I know of, mainly because during the depression years it seems we had the biggest crop of sweet potatoes ever grown. The sorghum crop was good, too. I never got tired of sweet potatoes and molasses, although I never eat either of them now. What I'm doing is just laying off of 'em so they'll taste good again in case we have another depression.

On Sundays we generally had something extra, like new-ground turnips and cold coon, with delicious rabbit salad.

There are people who seem to want another depression. They say people would be happier and wouldn't live in a continuous rush all the time. Maybe they're right, but as for me, I prefer to be in a little bit of a rush and sort of unhappy like I am now.

VII

Be Yourself, Unless You're A Nut

The Good Lord gave everybody some kind of talent. Many of 'em got the same kind but he gave everybody a different style and he certainly didn't intend for 'em to adopt somebody else's. Actually, it's just like stealing.

Sometimes it's hard not to believe that Darwin was right about that monkey business, especially when we see so many Americans trying to act like somebody else making a flop out of it.

Every day on the streets you'll see a lot of pretty girls going around trying to look like Marilyn Monroe. Some of 'em do have some of her features, but they would look a lot better acting

HOW NOT TO WORRY ABOUT

like plain Daisy Brown or Mary Smith. Speaking of Marilyn, I have yet to see a picture of her where she didn't have her mouth wide open. These girls I'm talking about keep their mouths open just like Marilyn, which certainly isn't healthful on account of the dust and insects we have around here.

This generation isn't the only one guilty of imitating others. Remember back years ago when Mae West was at the height of her popularity? Nearly every middle-aged woman in the country set out to capture some of Miss West's charm and you would see 'em walk down the street with their hips taking up so much sidewalk room you had to pass 'em when they got somewhere between neutral and over-drive. I still think that's where the car manufacturers got the idea of the new kind of shift.

If you're pretty enough to look like some famous movie star you'll be a lot prettier and attract more attention looking like yourself. Use your own style. It'll be fresher.

About half the young men we see on the amateur shows try to sing like Johnny Ray, Eddie Fisher, Pat Boone, or Elvis Presley. Johnny Ray would probably be an unknown singer, but he felt like crying when he sang so he broke down and cried and the public liked it. However, one crying crooner is sure a plenty. Develop your own style. By the time you get in the money, if you're good, the public will be sick and tired of the ones we have now. In fact, I'm tired of 'em already. Elvis Presley did that and he's doing pretty good for a country boy. Don't try to imitate him, though. This country, big and strong as it is, can stand only one. Every now and then I get to thinking we can't stand him.

We Americans have always been big imitators. Several years ago the University of Alabama had a great passing star named Harry Gilmer. He could jump high into the air, with men all around him, and get off a bullet-like pass good for fifty yards. High school football players saw him and for five years every high school passer in the country had to jump up four feet before they would chunk the ball. Maybe there wouldn't be anybody within ten yards of 'em, but they just simply had to jump anyhow. They never were able to hit their receivers like Gilmer but they could jump just as high and that seemed to be the main thing.

Years ago we heard countless evangelists try to imitate Billy Sunday, Gypsy Smith, and many of the other great preachers. None of 'em could put it over and they would have been far more effective had they used the style that God gave 'em. Billy Graham has proved that simple, plain preaching gets far better results. He preaches just like Billy Graham.

Try to imitate somebody and you'll get your own style mixed up with somebody else's and it'll be a mess. There's a big difference between emulating and imitating.

VIII

Don't Hold The Phone, Unless You're Strong

Monday morning, a little bright and entirely too early, my phone rang loud and long. It had to ring loud to get me aroused and it had to ring long to give me time to feel around for the phone.

In order to get one of those cheery, been-up-an-hour notes in my voice I hesitated before saying what I'm afraid was a very gruff "hello."

"Are you the Mr. Tucker who does carpentering work?" a very cordial, mellow and feminine voice asked.

"No, I'm sorry," I answered, not knowing yet what I was sorry about. "However, if you'll hold the phone just a minute

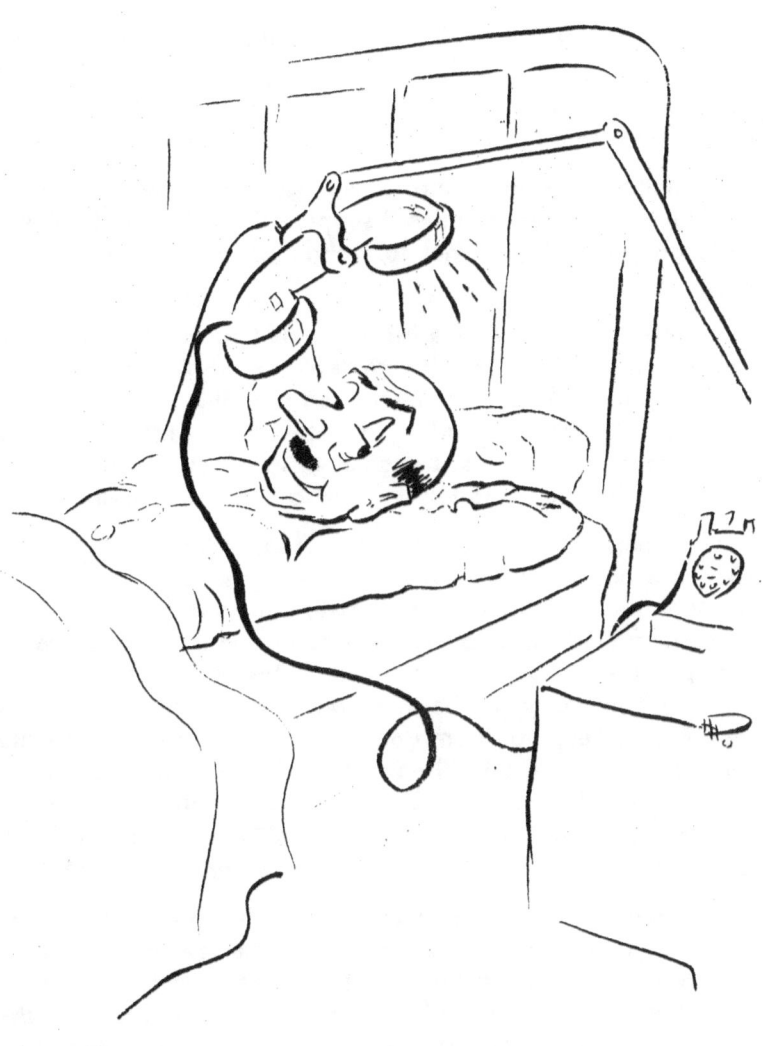

I'll look in the directory and see what the Mr. Tucker's phone number who is a carpenter is." My English is always a little worse early in the morning. The lady said she would be glad to hold the phone.

Calmly, deliberately and slowly I got out of bed and dress-ed, after which I went to town. I suppose the lady is still holding the phone. Sometimes I get to wondering if I'm meaner than other people.

Carpentering heads the list of things I know nothing about. It even comes ahead of Alabama's Minimum School Program. To me a hammer is an instrument used to obliterate finger prints on fingers. A saw is a gadget used to rip the legs off trousers and a plane is a machine designed to take huge chunks out of a board when you try to take off just a little thin shaving.

The best years of my life were spent trying to fix a cedar chest that had a broken base on one corner, causing it to tilt over with the slightest weight. Screws, nails and glue were tried but nothing worked. If you ever get to feeling the least bit cocky and up-in-the-world, try to fix a cedar chest. It'll take you down a peg or two and you'll be meek and humble for weeks there-after. But, to keep you from going to all the trouble and saying a lot of bad words, I'll tell you how I finally fixed mine. I put a brick under the corner and it works nicely. If you're finicky you can paint the brick a color to match the rest of the base. Better still, knock off the other three corners and use four bricks.

People shouldn't complain about the prices carpenters charge anymore than they should about the fees a doctor or a lawyer charges. It must have taken carpenters just as long to learn to drive a nail as it did a doctor to learn to prescribe the proper pill or for a lawyer to learn how to plead, answer and demur, or whatever they do. It fascinates me to watch a man drive a nail who really knows how. If I fail to hit a nail square on the head, it flies to a far corner of the room. If I do hit it right, the nail bends.

If you must have some carpentering work done around the house, get a carpenter to do it. Carpenters are busy people nowadays, though, and if you can get by at all without calling one, try to do it. And you can get by without one, provided you know a few simple little tricks. Some planks on my front porch had rotted out, but I saved a carpenter's bill by placing a Coca-Coal icebox over the missing planks. Then there was the hole in the bathroom wall that looked very unsightly. Some people would have called in a man to fix it, but I simply placed Aunt Sadie's picture over it—her face to the wall. This saves me the trouble of turning the picture around when I take a bath. Aunt Sadie was always so nice.

Doors that drag on the floor can be fixed with a little time. You simply take the hinges off and put the door in the basement. If you have a door that has too much daylight at the bottom stuff the paper containing this column under it.

IX

You Can Lighten Your Brother's Load By Carrying His Bullets

Last week in Florida a 79-year-old man shot a bartender who tried to help him off the floor. Another guy tried to take the pistol away from the old man and he got shot too. It took 10 men and some highway patrolmen to subdue the fellow.

There are lots of old people who resent younger people trying to help them in any way. They don't like for you to help them out of chairs or up steps or across the street. Some of 'em will tell you so mighty quick while others will kind of brush you

36

back, politely but firmly. Maybe I'll feel differently when I'm
79, but right now I think I would rather like being helped. Like
it is, I'm at the "awkward stage" in life. I'm often too tired to
get up for a drink of water but I'm not old enough to ask somebody to bring it to me. Sometimes, after sitting in one position
for an hour or two, it puts me in a powerful strain to get up,
but nobody would ever think of helping me on account of I'm
not quite old enough. Maybe if I can make it a few more years
I'll get a little sympathy. People might even offer to tote my
gun when I'm in the woods hunting, which would sure be nice.
I'd let 'em tote it, too.

Of course, we deplore barroom fighting, on account of most
anybody can get hurt, especially innocent bystanders. In fact, it's
the worst place in the world for an innocent bystander to be.
Everybody starts hitting the fellow nearest to him, whether he's
in the fight or not. What you do when a fight breaks out is to
grab a long, black beer-bottle, and when you catch somebody
looking the other way, you let him have it. Right about that
time somebody is going to catch you looking the other way
and you're going to get one busted over your head too. Old
experienced barroom fighters always rush to a corner the minute
a fight breaks out, but this method affords safety to only four
people as there are only four corners.

Back in my drinking days I discovered that strong drink
affected people three different ways. Some people, when they
get too much to drink, want to fight. Others love everybody
and they'll often break down and cry telling their friends, or
anybody else, how much they love 'em. Others want to sing.
This is the worst type, and I always tried to avoid this group.
I didn't mind fighting a little and I could put up with a fellow
telling me how much he liked me and what a fine fellow I was,
but I never could stand a drunk trying to sing. It's something
awful. They kind of warble like, and they inject a few vocal
tears into songs about Mothers, Old Pals of Mine and I'll be

Carried to the New Jail Tomorrow. Sometimes I think our most ardent prohibitionists got that way from hearing a bunch of drunks try to sing.

Too, there are three different types of drinkers. We have the social drinker, who takes a nip every now and then thinking it might help him get an order or get elected Governor or something. They don't actually like the taste of whiskey, but they are a bad influence on everybody else. People see them take one or two drinks and they think maybe they can drink that way, too. Later they find out they can't. We have next the spree drinker. He gets drunk about four times a year and stays on it for a couple of weeks. The reason he gets drunk only four times a year is because he can't stand it physically or financially any oftener. It takes about three months for him to get in shape for another one. Then we have the steady drinker who staggers only when he gets stone-cold sober.

All three types are bad. Any of 'em are liable to bust out singing all of a sudden.

38

X

Millionaires Should Wear Badges

They say a man is old when he quits dreaming of things he would like to do and things he would like to be. If that is true, I'm still a young man.

Maybe I've had more than my share of dreams during the half century I've been around, but I remember them all very vividly. When I was of the apron-string age, I hoped some day I would grow up and operate the flat-bed, horse-drawn public dray that brought things to our house from the stores downtown. The driver looked very comfortable and rested sitting on an apple box and his work carried him to all parts of the town every day.

When I was a little older I saw my first train and envied the engineer who, every day, traveled that route from Selma to Mobile. I dreamed I was up there in the cabin, operating the black, iron monster, blowing the whistle, ringing the bell, letting off steam just when I got to a crowd of people beside the tracks. I could picture myself, waving to farmers in the fields and to pretty young girls standing on their porches. In fact, I'm still a little disappointed because I never got to ride in the locomotive of one of the steam-driven engines.

Somehow, I missed dreaming of becoming President of the United States. Maybe it was because I never did think much of Presidents or maybe I never did like the idea of holding a job where half the people bragged on you and the other half gave you down the country. It's much nicer being in a business where everybody gives you down the country.

At the age of ten, or thereabouts, I picked out my life's work again. I would become a soda-jerk, eat ice cream, drink chocolate milks and flirt with the girls who came in the drug store. This ambition, too, soon died, and I decided I would just as soon be another Walter Johnson or Christy Mathewson. In case some of you young people have never heard of these re-nowned athletes, let me say that they were the top pitchers in the major leagues just a few years back. Well, maybe just a little further back. Unfortunately for me and the baseball world, though, I never got much practice pitching on account of another boy's parents had more money than mine and he furnished the baseball, which settled that.

Not realizing my ambition to become a big-league pitcher didn't bother me too much, because in the meantime I had de-cided to become a movie actor like Wallace Reid or William S. Hart and It's none of you young squirt's business who they were. I reckon what made me decide to get in the movies was because

THE LOVE LIFE OF SPIDERS

I was so handsome and had such a fine personality. I was i
a school play, though, and after it was over I waited around fui
the audience to rush forward and congratulate me on my sterling
performance but, instead, they made a rush for the exit. Just a
little encouragement on their part right at that time and I might
have become one of our country's greatest actors.

Later, the idea of being a millionaire kind of appealed to
me and that is probably what I should have become. I can't
think of anybody who could do a better job. It seems to me that
millionaires should wear a large badge of some kind, saying
"Millionaire." Like it is, some of 'em you can't hardly tell from
anybody else. They go around acting like ordinary folks and
most of 'em can fumble around about reaching for a check as
well as I can.

Well, here I am, 50 years and a thousand dreams older,
and I haven't realized any of my ambitions. Maybe I'm starting on my second childhood, but I kind of think now that operating a public, horse-drawn dray might still be my best bet. There
isn't much demand for a dray of that type and business never
would be rushing. A fellow, at least, could get off a few days
without worrying about what was happening back home.

Even Skunks Can Smile At Their Neighbors

Somehow or other it's hard for me to get heated up over the National Friendship Week we have just gone through. The reason, I reckon, is that too many people I know are not capable of properly celebrating the event. Too many people know too little about the meaning of friendship. It's not like Christmas. Everybody celebrates Christmas and that's what makes it so popular. Some get drunk and some go to Church. Some fight and some get married, after which they fight some more. Some give and some gouge. But it's celebrated, anyway, and everybody looks forward to Christmas.

THE LOVE LIFE OF SPIDERS

Don't get me wrong—I'm not opposed to Friendship Week. It just seems that it's a mighty short period to devote to anything so important. It takes a week to get friendly enough with your neighbor to borrow his lawn mower. You can't get to know a man well enough in seven days to gossip about people you want to gossip about because you don't know who all he's kin to. Of course, gossiping shouldn't be the basis of true friendship, but it does draw people closer together when they have a mutual acquaintance they both think is a you-know-what.

Too, some people might join in the observance of the Week and then go about being perfect snobs for the remainder of the year, thinking they had fulfilled their obligation for the entire year just because they sent their neighbor a bowl of strawberries and two slices of cake. You know, some people are like that. They do one little nice thing and then go around with one of those "obligation paid" looks on their faces for the next twelve months. Some people might even return the garden hose they borrowed last summer and call themselves celebrating Friendship Week.

But, seeing as how we already have the Week set apart, make it mean something worthwhile. To begin with, we should all learn the difference between friendliness and Friendship, and there is one whale of a difference. A fellow can pass you in a car and see you out sweating trying to change a flat tire and wave at you and yell howdy. He's a friendly fellow, but the man who stops and helps you change the tire is a friend. See the difference? When you have trouble a friendly fellow will tell you to just let him know if he can be of any assistance. The friend will go ahead and help you without your asking.

In order to get something out of this special week, try to figure out ways you can prove your friendship. Maybe the neighbors would like to see a show once in a while, but can't leave the baby. Make it a point to keep the baby every now and then, even if he is a spoiled little brat. You might be able to give him a sound whipping without his parents ever knowing about it.

HOW NOT TO WORRY ABOUT

There are so many ways to be a friend. You can refrain from showing visitors the family photos when they visit you and leave off Junior's piano rendition of "Dance of The Rose Buds." Too, it isn't necessary to remind Mrs. Smyth that she always looks good in that particular hat, with emphasis on the "always."

And it's nice to visit your acquaintances several nights during the year. It makes them so happy when you leave. Maybe I can make you happy right now by cutting this column short.

XII

State Budgets And Hound Dogs

It has been suggested that I write a column about the advisability of Alabama selecting an "official" state dog. It's a splendid idea for a column but I don't think much of it as far as the dog business is concerned.

Alabama has made such a mess of selecting "official" things that I'm mighty afraid we might wind up with a pot-likker hound. Take our state flower, the goldenrod, for instance. Actually, I don't believe it's a flower in the first place. What I think it is is a weed. It is generally found growing along with the ragweed, which is guilty of bringing on attacks of sneezing to hay-fever sufferers. I wouldn't like the goldenrod, even if it were pretty. It keeps the wrong kind of company.

HOW NOT TO WORRY ABOUT

Maybe you don't know it, but our state has an "official" fish. It's the tarpon, which is found in all parts of the state except in that particular region known as Alabama. The average fellow in Clarke County wouldn't recognize a tarpon if he met one in the big road. If Alabama has to have an "official" fish which I very much doubt, it should be the catfish. Negroes first discovered the delicious flavor of fried catfish but, being smart, they didn't say anything about it for a long time on account of they didn't want the white folks to eat it all up. Finally, though, it got out how good it was and most everybody likes it.

The catfish is found in every section of Alabama, whereas I'll bet you could fish the entire length of Hal's Lake until you were blue in the face and never catch a tarpon. You might catch one out in the Gulf of Mexico, 20 miles or so from Mobile, but when you do you're actually worse off. They aren't fit to eat and you'll have the thing mounted and your friends, everytime they come to visit you, will have to listen to you tell how it pulled and fought and all that.

Our "official" state bird is the yellowhammer, which is a fair weather friend, and when it gets cold he checks out for a warmer section. A yellowhammer ain't nothing but a woodpecker in technicolor.

I reckon the Federation of Music Clubs will get mad with me, but I don't think so powerfully much of our "official" state song, "Alabama." It sounds pretty bad as a song and as a poem it leaves me kind of flat, especially that part where, "From thy Southern shores, where groweth, by the sea the orange tree." It's all right except that we don't have a sea and we don't have orange trees. Then, over in the second stanza the lady has poor give-out Moses climbing "lone Nebo's Mount to see, Alabama, Alabama, we will aye be true to thee." I never could figure out how Moses got in the act. Seems like she could nave let Moses climb Birmingham's Vulcan where he could have seen more in a shorter time.

THE LOVE LIFE OF SPIDERS

There's something bad wrong with the tune. Last night I tried singing the song to the tune of "Blueberry Hill" but it sounded worse. Next I tried using "Mona Lisa" but that didn't work either. Tonight, if my neighbors are away from home, I'm going to try using the "Green Door" tune. I believe it'll work.

When we get around to picking out a state dog we're liable to get in bad trouble. You have to automatically eliminate the hound dog on account of Tennessee having a prior claim. We'll also eliminate the Dachshund because they're built so close to the floor you can't tell if they're fixing to kick a piece of furniture and you don't have time to yell at 'em.

That still leaves a wide variety from which to choose. Noah must have had a lot of trouble. (If they can get Moses mixed up in a state song I reckon I can use Noah in a column.) If he got two each of every species on that ark he sure had a boat-load.

Some people will almost fight when they get in a discussion involving the merits of various dogs so we had sure better go slow in making a final decision.

If anybody gets mad about what I've written in this column I'll certainly make a public apology. I still think, though, we can get along without an "official" state dog.

Don't Fear Ghosts Unless They're Real

I have always found it difficult to overcome the superstitions I picked up as a child. My parents were not superstitious, but an old woman came to our house every Monday to help with the weekly washing and, as a child of four or five, I liked to "help" keep the fire going under the big iron washpot. It was on those Mondays that I learned most of the bad-luck omens.

For instance, when a cedar tree gets as high as the top of a house, somebody in the house is sure to die. Although I learned this from her, I have since found that many apparantly sensible people believe the same thing. There is some basis for their belief, but it is a natural one. It probably takes a cedar tree forty years to reach house-top height and during that span somebody in the house is apt to die of old age, if of nothing else.

I learned from her that by turning a somersault upon hearing the first whippoorwill of Spring, good luck would follow me throughout the year. For some twenty years I did just that, but here lately, if I attempted a somersault, I would have to enjoy my good luck from a hospital bed with my back in a brace.

Asafetida (I looked up the spelling) hung around the neck was supposed to keep off some kind of disease, but I'm not sure what it was. The only thing I remember that it effectively kept off was people.

For years I believed that a Rabbit crossing the road, from right to left, was an omen of bad things to come. Of course, it's silly to let a thing like that worry you, when all you have to do is to turn your hat around for the next mile.

Many of the beliefs of a hundred years ago have been debunked. Applicants for insurance policies were often turned down because they "used no whisky." Prior to that many women were burned at the stake because they were thought to be witches and able to practice witchcraft. We still have plenty of witches but we've quit burning them. What we do now is marry them and let 'em wear sack dresses. We've made some progress in this line. They've quit carrying a broom.

Ptomaine poison (I looked that up, too) was something to be dreaded forty years ago. It was caused, they thought, by eating food out of a can. Mama was so afraid of us taking it that she opened the cans upside down so she could get the food on a platter faster. Now it's common knowledge that you can keep opened canned food for six months if it's kept under refrigeration.

Some of the old superstitions were based on good horse sense. It's certainly not a good idea to walk under a ladder on account of somebody might drop a hammer or a bucket of paint on your head. It's not wise to light three cigarettes off of one match because you can get your fingers burned. A bowl of water kept under the bed was supposed to reduce fever. Of course it didn't but it was a fine thing to have if the house caught fire.

What I'm wondering is that maybe some of the things they're telling us nowadays are pure baloney. It could be that people a hundred years from now will laugh at us for thinking cigarettes cause lung cancer. Well, anyway, it's something nice to think about.

Seeing as how we've come so far, it seems we could find easier ways to spell asafetida, ptomaine and pneumonia.

XIV

Photographers Should Charge Less For Pretty People

A friend who sees my picture in one of the dailies using this column writes that it doesn't do me justice. He is very kind and I want him to know I am truly grateful.

Somehow, photographers have never been able to catch my handsomeness on film. When I have a picture made the photographer gets more or less careless. What I think happens is that they see how good looking I am and get over confident.

It seems to me, though, that it's better to use a picture that doesn't look so good, because then people will say you look much better than your picture. People are always telling me that I'm not nearly as ugly as my picture would indicate. Of course they may not mean a word of it. Some people are always trying to say nice things.

A photographer scares me just about as much as a dentist. Both of 'em have a lot in common, when it comes to dealing with me. A dentist hurts me physically and the photographer hurts my pride.

Quite a few people, though, seem like they enjoy having frequent pictures made. In later years these same pictures will afford the children a great deal of amusement on rainy days when they have to stay in. They'll laugh and giggle at papa and mama in those ridiculous styles. It's quite a problem to decide what kind of clothes to wear when you have a picture made. Whatever you wear will be out of style within a few short years and you'll wonder if you really ever thought those silly clothes were pretty. Of all the photos I ever had made, only one has the modern look. It was made by my father when I was three months old. There has been no change in the style I wasn't wearing.

Most parents spend as much money on having their first baby photographed as they spend on baby food. By the time some of 'em are two years old they're ready to go on television.

There is an old Chinese proverb which says one picture is worth a thousand words. If that's true I'm personally in favor of fewer words. I'm not blaming the photographers for the way I look, but they should take part of the responsibility. For instance, they get me focused just right and I'm in a powerful strain but instead of flashing the bulb and flipping the do-dad, they look real pitiful like and come around to get one of my shoulders up or down. Then they start all over. When I think they're all set, they pull something out of the camera and take

THE LOVE LIFE OF SPIDERS

another peep. Things don't look so good, so they come around the second time, straighten up my tie, push me further back on the stool and move two of the lights. By this time perspiration is popping all over my greatly extended forehead and to keep people from thinking I'm a working man, I wipe it off. Naturally, I'm off-side or something so they have to re-focus me all over.

Again, they're ready and ask for a big smile. It seems to me there is very little to smile about. I'm nervous and they're nervous and I'm thinking about the ten bucks or more the picture is going to cost me and how it's going to look. But I do try to smile. I put my mind on beautiful things, like pork chops, bluegills, a platter full of chitterlings, and a pair of aces. Finally, I do smile, but it isn't the spontaneous smile they want. It's the forced type like you see a fellow wearing when he goes to the front door and sees his mother-in-law there with three suitcases.

Eventually, however, I get tickled thinking how silly it is for me, a grown man, to be sitting there having a picture made and I break out into a very fine and wholesome smile. Then in a few days I get four "proofs." They call 'em proofs because it simply proves what I had already suspected. I'm instructed to pick out the best one, which I do by showing 'em to my friends. The one they laugh at least I take. There's no such thing as justice from a photographer.

Adam Missed His Mother-In-Law

I n Chicago a woman is being sued for $300,000 by her son's wife. In the suit it was claimed that the mother-in-law "designed wickedly, maliciously, intentionally and wantonly to overcome the devotion and love of her husband." It was also claimed that the mother-in-law persuaded her husband to desert and abandon her and that they would have been a happy, loving couple had it not been for the "constant interference" in their lives.

Now $300,000 is a pretty good chunk of money and I imagine the case will be watched with considerable interest throughout the entire country. If the mother-in-law has to pay off I wouldn't be at all surprised to see several hundred cases

54

filed right here in our town. Even the threat of a suit would be a good weapon to hold over the head of the mother-in-law if she barged in for an extended visit and started in upsetting the household. You could start threatening her about the second week.

Actually, there are two kinds of mothers-in-law. One is the wife's mother and the other is the husband's mother. The husband's mother is the worst, because she is the one who cooked such good biscuits, tender roasts and delicious pies. She is the one, who, for 20 years, went around picking up his clothes, seeing that his shirts were laundered just so and having his suits cleaned and pressed when they needed it. She is the villian who caused him to be a spoiled brat.

The wife's mother, in the eyes of the husband, is an old she-demon because she is always hinting around that he should provide better for his loving wife and not make of her an ordinary slave.

Mothers-in-law are kidded so much that I think it's time somebody came to their rescue. There aren't nearly as many mean mothers-in-law as there are mean sons-and-daughters-in-law.

Maybe some of 'em are mean and meddiesome and ornery, but it's strange to me that no one ever makes jokes about fathers-in-law. Maybe they're just smarter or more adroit with their meddling, but I reckon grandfathers spoil more grandchildren than all the parents, aunts and uncles put together. They'll laugh and tell their friends about Junior saying something they would have beat heck out of their own son for saying.

I made a survey once to find out for myself what men really thought about their mothers-in-law. I interviewed ten men, asking each one point-blank for their opinion, and the results were astounding. Six of the ten, a clear majority, said they loved 'em and didn't see how they could get along without 'em. They mentioned as good qualities such things as free baby sitting, financial help at times and excellent counsel in times of marital discord.

Two said they were very fond of 'em, but could manage somehow to get along without one if the worst came to the worst. One said his had passed on several months prior to my interveiw and he didn't look like a man who had spent a great amount of time grieving. What the tenth one said couldn't be printed on ordinary newsprint. Eight out of ten speaking out for them, though, is a pretty good indication that they are pretty well thought of, even if we do joke about them.

This case in Chicago I don't know anything about. Maybe the old lady did bust up the marriage, but I'll tell you right now, if the gal can swap him off for $300,000 she sure ain't made a bad deal any way you figure it.

XVI

You Can't Take It With You --But Then, Who's Leaving?

A friend of mine suggested I write a column about the advantages of being poor. This is going to be a powerfully short column this week. I would much prefer being in a position to write about the disadvantages of being rich, whatever they are.

About the only advantage of being poor, the way I see it, is that you don't have much to lose. Then, if you do lose what you've got, it doesn't take long to build your fortune back up to what it was. A fellow who lost a million dollars nowadays,

HOW NOT TO WORRY ABOUT

with taxes like they are, would probably never be able to make another million, whereas a man who never had over $30 could get well by Saturday night.

There are rich people who act like they're poor and there are poor people who act like they're rich. I feel sorry for both groups. The fellow who really enjoys life is the fellow who is poor, knows he's poor, and knows he's going to stay poor. That's me.

Lots of people fight against poverty all of their lives. Me, I fight against wealth. If I think I'm about to accumulate a little money I buy another outboard motor and a new fishing rod. It must be terrible to be sock up in the middle of a bream bed and start worrying about what General Motors stock is doing. When a fellow gets to the point where he had rather hear a cash register ring than to hear a fish break water he's a goner.

A poor man doesn't have to worry about getting his Cadillac scratched up. He's able to enjoy his '52 jalopy, and a few more dents and scratches here and there don't matter. He knows his wife married him for love and love alone, and he also knows that if she ever quits him, there won't be any question of how much alimony he has to pay.

Too many people let their business run them instead of them running the business. One of the smartest fellows I ever knew was a commercial fisherman who started off with one trot line. Catfish were bringing a pretty good price so he added two more lines and stayed busy most of the time. The last time I saw him, though, he had gone back to just one trot line. Said his business got too big for him.

Another fellow I knew was, at one time, just about the happiest man in the world. He had a beat-up truck with all the fenders off and the top was kind-of caved in and he would go around the country picking up scrap iron. People felt sort of sorry for him on account of the way he dressed and they just

58

gave him whatever scrap iron they had around the place. Well, he would work a few days and fish and hunt a few days and he made just enough to get by, but he was happy. Finally, though, he put in a scrap-iron yard and started buying the stuff from other dealers. His business got bigger and bigger and he bought a new truck and started wearing nice clothes and people started charging him for the scrap-iron instead of giving it to him and finally he went busted. Well, he had got used to being rich and he never was happy again as long as he lived.

Some people have a fear of not having any money in their old age, so they keep on working hard and saving hard, but they generally fail to get old. If I were a young man, starting all over, I think I'd study to become a retired mail carrier with a working wife. There ain't no better set-up than that.

Time never drags for a poor man. A rich man is looking forward to monthly coupon cutting and dividend checks, and to him the months roll around at a snail's pace. The poor man has installment payments coming due every month and time really flies. If you don't believe it, sign up for a TV set, air conditioner, automobile, washing machine and refrigerator.

When a doctor tells a rich man he should quit work and rest, he gets another doctor. If a doctor tells a poor man to quit work and rest, he kisses the doctor.

In fact, I like everything about being a poor man except not having any money. It certainly is a serious drawback.

XVII

The Finance Company Already Has A Refrigerator

Time must have passed mighty slow-like back in the tough old days before they had such a thing as installment buying. That was way back when cafes cut a pie in four pieces and nobody had ever heard of a woman short-stop.

Installment buying really makes time fly. Most families have a car note due on the 10th, a payment on the refrigerator due on the 15th. On the 20th we scrap up enough to keep the washing machine and then make arrangements on the 25th to

THE LOVE LIFE OF SPIDERS

meet the T.V. payment. On the 1st we just throw away our money on foolishness like groceries and house rent. Psychologists say we are happiest when time passes rapidly. If that's true, installment buying has caused me to become just about giggling crazy, or note happy.

People back in the old days couldn't have had much, because mighty few people ever get far enough ahead to plank down cash for what they buy. Too, there must have been a lot of un-employment back then. They didn't have service stations, which meant that at least twenty million people didn't have jobs. All of 'em couldn't have worked at livery stables, because we never have had that many horses. Whole horses, that is.

Not only the months, but the years pass too fast when you sign up for something on those "12 Easy Payments" which you learn later includes interest at goodness only knows what rate of interest, plus insurance and plus one or two other things that you never quite figure out. Actually, though, I feel very kindly toward the finance people. They have enabled me to own many things I could have never thought of owning had it not been for them. All that I have, or ever expect to own, I owe to the darling E-Z Payment and Repossessing Corporation. Too, they have kept me at work. Lots of times I couldn't go hunting because I had to stay on the job so I could make enough money to meet the payment on my shotgun. Lots of time I couldn't go fishing because I might not have enough cash to meet the next note on my outboard motor. They have made me enjoy the hot summers, because it is then I pay for my floor furnace. They have made me enjoy the cold winter nights, because I am meeting payments 9, 10, and 11 on my room air-conditioner.

There is another kind of installment buying known as the "Lay-Away Plan." This never did appeal to me in the least, because the merchant puts all the worrying off on the customer. You don't get the merchandise until you have made all the payments. Seems to me like both parties to a transaction should get in on the worrying deal. If I'm going to worry about something I want to be using it enough to compensate for the worrying I do. Under this plan, the merchant lays it away and you lay awake trying to figure out how you're going to make the next payment. Maybe it·should be called the "Lay-Awake Plan."

During my long years of experience in installment buying, however, I have found that the finance people are really nice guys. They aren't nearly so cold-blooded as their collection letters 2, 3, and 4 would indicate. If you don't think they're friendly and polite, just fail to send in your next payment for a couple of months. They'll drop around for a chat and to your amazement you'll learn that the last thing they want is your refrigerator and washing machine. They already have some.

XVIII

Just Because You're A Ripe Old Age Doesn't Mean It's Plucking Time

A publishing house frequently sends me literature about a little booklet called, "How To Grow Old Gracefully." Somebody must have sent 'em my name, suggesting that I was growing old and maybe insinuating I wasn't doing it so gracefully.

The part about "How To Grow Old" appeals to me very much. It is something I'm powerfully interested in doing. I want to live to be an old man, and then hang around and finally get to be an old, old man. Fact is, I'd like to live to be so old I

HOW NOT TO WORRY ABOUT

could call a 90-year-old man "Kid."

That stuff about "Growing Old Gracefully" doesn't interest me much, but if somebody will write a book about how to grow old without rheumatism, or how to grow old without breaking a hip, they will probably find me very much in the market.

There's so much to live for nowadays. Some of these days the American public is going to rise up and put a stop to singing commercials. There may be bloodshed, but it will be worth the price to be able to eat a piece of bread or smoke a cigaret or shave without thinking of some ghastly song.

Another reason I would like to live to be an old man is because maybe some of these days our law-makers will sit down and try to think of some way to reduce taxes instead of constantly trying to think up new things to tax. Maybe, too, some of our state department heads might come before a legislative finance committee and say they can get by on half of what they've been getting and will they please decrease the appropriation. I must be getting old and senile already for even thinking of such a thing, because something like that will never happen.

Maybe by the time I'm old and decrepit I might be able to drive over a farm-to-market road that really goes some place. All I've ever seen so far went six miles and stopped at nowhere. You start changing gears at the market and by the time you're in high you've reached the farm and have to get back in low to get through the mud to reach another six-mile strip going to another market.

Right now I'm interested in the ultimate results of our peace talks with Russia. Maybe in the next fifty years we'll get a pretty good idea of whether they're going to fight or not. Too, I would like tc see France change her form of government. Under the system they use now, it works kind of like the PTA. Nobody wants to be president of the PTA or premier of France. The only difference is that you can't get rid of the PTA presidency and in

THE LOVE LIFE OF SPIDERS

France you can't keep the premiership. You can't expect a school child to know who's head of their government unless he listened to the early morning news.

Yes, sir, there are just lots of things that make me want to live on and on. The way I figure it now, unless I have some bad luck, I'll be plum out of debt when I reach age 90, and I would like to walk down the street without having to cross over to avoid one of my creditors. Some people manage to duck into a building when they see somebody coming they owe, but I can't do that. I owe somebody in all the buildings.

And then, along about 1995, it would be nice to sit on the front porch in a comfortable rocking chair and have the Welfare Director send me my monthly old-age check and be able to fuss because it's not quite as much as one of my neighbors is getting.

Grow old? Yes. Gracefully - Well, not too gracefully. We kind of overlook it when little children are mischievous and get in trouble, but we think it's something awful for an old man to get mixed up in some kind of scandal. Personally, I hope I get caught in a night spot raid at the age of 96 and have the judge give me a good lecture about what's becoming of the future generation.

But when the Good Lord feels like I've enjoyed this world long enough, I would like for Him to find me resting at noontime on the banks of Hal's Lake, with a boat cushion under my head and a beat-up hat over my eyes. I would like to go to sleep there with the sound of squirrels chattering in the huge oaks overhead and the fish breaking the cool, clear water of the nearby stream.

XIX

Is It Proper To Open A Closed Checking Account?

There was a fellow through our town a while back selling check protector machines. What he would do was to enter a business establishment and get the proprietor to write him a check for $4.00. He would then take the check in the presence of the boss, and raise it to either $40 or $400. This would scare the boss so badly that he would order a machine right away and lots ot times he was scared to write another check until he got the protector in operation.

The salesman never could get far trying to sell me one,

though. I have a much better system and one that has never failed. The bank looks out for any check raising that might be done on checks I have sent out. When and if a crook raises one of my four-dollar checks to $400, he is just out $4. In fact, several years ago, some transient crook picked up a bunch of our printed checks and for the next five or six weeks they came in from all over the South. The bank turned down most of 'em without even detecting the forgery. They were going by the amounts of the checks and the balance on my ledger sheet.

Seems like everybody has something to worry about. The people with big bank balances worry about check-raising artists and us poor folks worry about whether the ones we write will be paid as is. I don't know which type worrying is the worst, but I sure would like to swap around for a few years and find out.

Seems like a fellow would get accustomed to poverty after going through fifty years of it, but I still don't like it. The main objection I have to poverty is that I don't have the money to buy the things I want to buy. Right now, with this pretty Spring weather, I would like very much to own one of the pretty new boats advertised in the daily papers. Instead, I'll probably have to go through another season with the home-made job I've been using for several years. It is bad about leaking and when I catch a fish and throw him in the boat, he splatters muddy water all over my clothes and gets my glasses where I can't see.

There is some good to all things, though, and my leaking boat has caused me to find a use for old razor blades, which is something that greater minds than mine have failed to do. I take the old dull and rusty blades and use 'em to stuff strips of old underwear in the cracks of the boat. This also provides a use for old underwear. For several years I used 'em as dish cloths at our camp, but some of the members are a little on the squeamish side. Maybe poverty, instead of necessity, is the mother of invention.

HOW NOT TO WORRY ABOUT

There are, of course, other advantages of poverty. Over the past 30 years I have come to know a fine group of finance company collectors, and I expect I call at least a hundred of 'em by their first names. Some of us even swap Christmas cards. As a rule, they are mighty fine people, and after you get to know 'em, you learn that when they say they're going to repossess a refrigerator if they don't get a check for payment number 17 by Tuesday, they don't necessarily mean this oncoming Tuesday. What they mean is that they'll be back on that date so you can get together and pick out another Tuesday. They realize it's folks like us who keep 'em from having to haul paper wood for a living.

With all the above mentioned advantages of poverty, though, I sure would like to lay awake for a few nights worrying about some low-down varmint getting $400 for a $4 check.

XX

Would Nero Have Fiddled With A Flat Tire?

Returning home recently from a fishing trip, I discovered my conscience was bothering me a little. I had gone on the trip when I should have stayed at my office where work was piled up telephone high. On top of that I was worried about the fish not biting as they should have. That was worrying me considerable more than the work I had left undone, but both of 'em hitting me at the same time was kind of annoying. For years I have been an exponent of the unworried mind, but I reckon every man needs something to happen now and then to give him renewed faith in his philosophy of life.

That particular something was about to happen. The mercury was fraternizing with the 100 mark. The sun was beaming down and my clothes were wet with perspiration which also had me worried. My own sweat is something I can't bear to see.

As we drove around a curve on the lonely dusty road, we saw a fellow sitting on the fender of his car which was parked just off the road right in the blazing sun and he was picking on a guitar! He actually was, and he was singing mournful like about a gal who had crossed up some guy by going off with some other guy. It was a real sad tune, and the man was putting his whole heart in it.

He had a flat tire, and he didn't have a jack, and even if he had had one it wouldn't have done him any good because he didn't have a spare. Guess he had to leave the spare at home to make room for his guitar. He never did fully quit plunking on it all the time we were there. I reckon he was the most unworried man I ever saw. He figured, I reckon, there was't much he could do about an impossible situation, so he did the only logical thing under the circumstances: he just gave a git-tar concert to himself.

There wasn't much we could do to help the fellow. My spare wouldn't fit his wheel so there wasn't any need of jacking it up which suited me just fine, because I believe the fellow would have let me do all the work. If and when I change a tire on a hot day, there sure ain't going to be nobody looking at me work while they're sitting on a fender playing a git-tar.

Seeing as how I couldn't help him, I said maybe I had better be moving along. It didn't seem to bother him, me leaving him there alone. He just said, "That's O.K. Somebody will come along pretty soon and everything will be all right." As I drove off he crawled back up on the fender and started back to singing and playing about the gal who left her man. I'm still wondering if the gal ever came back.

THE LOVE LIFE OF SPIDERS

It's such a pity everybody doesn't have that man's outlook on life. Some people actually hunt for something to worry about, but here was a man with plenty of trouble and he wasn't worried at all. Of course, everybody doesn't have a git-tar, thank goodness, but everybody could have his philosophy of life. He could have walked to the nearest town, about ten miles away, or he could have worked himself into a frenzy, but he did neither. He just got out his git-tar and cut down on a consoling tune.

The poor fellow may still be there, but if he is, I'll bet he ain't worried none. Unless, maybe, he broke a git-tar string, and even then, maybe somebody came along with a spare string and everything's all right.

It's bad to have a flat, but here are a few helpful hints you might remember when it happens to you. If there are other occupants in the car there is nothing to worry about. While they're getting out the spare and the tools, you start looking for a chunk to scotch the wheels. Sometime you have to walk a quarter of a mile up or down the road and when you get back they'll probably have it fixed. If they haven't, you can always kill a little more time by rolling up your sleeves and checking on the emergency brake.

If your wife is along, that calls for more planning. In this event, you hide in the woods and let a passing motorist stop and change tires. It'll work every time if your wife is either real pretty or real pitiful-looking.

All the above hints are good, but I reckon, after all, the guitar method is best. Actually ninety-nine times out of a hundred, people aren't in as big a hurry as they think they are, and besides, guitar music is kind of restful like.

Even Ugly Ducklings Have Their Favorites

When you watch a boxing bout on television you automatically select your favorite. You can watch one of those "forum" programs, where the participants are discussing some issue you don't know or care a hill of beans about, yet you'll find yourself pulling for one side. It's the same way in baseball. Most fans are against the Yankees because they're too good and have been winning too long. They're against the Bums for a number of reasons, but it's mostly because of the wars.

Now you wonder how war got mixed up in baseball, but it's a fact. The soldiers Brooklyn sent to the war certainly didn't serve as ambassadors of good will. Ask any veteran why he's against the Bums and he'll say it's because he was in the same outfit with somebody from Brooklyn. Sometimes I think maybe our soldiers spent as much time fighting the Brooklynites as they did the Japs and Germans. What I think caused this unpopularity was because our soldiers just never did learn the language spoken by the boys from Brooklyn. Their language is quite different from that spoken in other parts of the United States. You could get the same effect by taking a 10-year old boy from the mountains of Tennessee, bringing him up in an Italian home with a French-Irish instructor and sending him to a Hungarian Sunday School.

Brooklyn undoubtedly isn't a city of charm and culture, but I've always kind of pulled for the Bums, on account of everybody else is against them. I'm the only friend they have in this section of the state. It's very unfortunate, too, that I'm a Dodger fan, on account of some of my so-called friends don't speak to me at all during the summer months. Being for the Bums is sort of like a politician being against home, mother, pets, Lincoln and the family doctor.

Winning or losing, the Bums have a colorful team. When you hear of a team having three men on base, you think they might score. With the Bums, though, you never know whether they're all on one base or not. They do some daring base-stealing, but you never know whether there's a runner already on the base they're trying to steal. They'll fight at the drop of a hat. If they aren't fighting opposing players they're fighting each other.

Right now it looks like the team will move to California, where they will become the Los Angeles Angels. They'll probably be called the Bum Angels. They're having to leave Brooklyn on account of the city of New York refusing to build them an adequate ball park. You see, Brooklyn doesn't have a Mayor or City Council like we do in Thomasville. If they had their own city government they could get more help. If they had a third baseman they could win more games.

So, like I say, we all pick out somebody to be for or against and we never know quite why we did. I reckon the reason I pull for the Dodgers is because the team is made up of such old men, and they have a lot of courage to get out there every day and risk getting a broken bone. Us old people have got to stick together. Youth is going to make it, regardless of whether we pull for 'em or not.

Besides, dem lousy Braves shud be throwed outda Nashul Leg.

Who Said That Silence Is Golden?

This column is reprinted in a number of papers over the state by editors who are trying to fill up space, and program chairmen are always trying to find somebody— just anybody—to fill up an hour-long program, so they invite me, hoping I'll be so bad they can maybe get fired from the program committee.

Anyway, they call me from all parts of Alabama, and I very quickly tell 'em I can't make a speech. They say I bet you can and I say I bet I can't and it gets down to a yes-you-can no-I-can't conversation with only Southern Bell getting any place.

Well, because of the many invitations I have received, I'm working up a speech and along about February I'm going to

THE LOVE LIFE OF SPIDERS

practice on the Dothan Rotary Club. I picked February because it's a cold, bleak and lousy month and nobody expects anything good to happen. I picked the Rotary because most Rotarians are so worried during February about the income tax they'll have to pay in March that they don't hear anything you say nohow. I selected Dothan because it's a long ways from Thomasville and it'll take longer for the reports of my speech to get back home.

There's just one thing about public speaking that bothers me: I get scared slap to death the minute I get up before a bunch of people. My hands seem to get scared too, and start looking for some place to hide. They jump around from place to place and I can't seem to control 'em properly. They get behind me, on the table in front of me, in my pockets, in my lapels, and I have a hard time getting one of 'em to use in scratching my nose, which always starts twitching about the time I say I'm powerfully glad to be here tonight, which I ain't. Fact is, I'd rather be most any place else, including Sniper Ridge, Old Baldy and Jane Russell Hill.

However, I'm looking forward to my speech in Dothan. When I was very little I got an almost sadistic pleasure out of tying tin cans and paper bags to our cat's tail. When a fellow grows up, though, he has to put away childish things, but he can still get the same kind of doubtful satisfaction out of watching an audience writhe and suffer. My speech to the Rotarians will probably be the finest thing that has ever happened to the Dothan Kiwanis Club.

The speech I'm working on isn't going to be deep and thought-provoking, though, like this column. It'll just be a bunch ot crazy stuff, and the only thing the audience will have to worry about is trying to tell their wives what I talked about. The trouble with lots of speeches I hear nowadays is that they get people upset. If they're too gloomy, people get to wonder-

ing what's going to happen to the country. If they're too opti-
mistic it gets 'em to wondering why they aren't doing better
themselves. My talk will accomplish both purposes: They'll suffer
for 20 minutes, and then they'll be happy that it's over.

Some of my friends have been offering helpful tips about
my speech. Some say I should try to imitate Will Rogers, but I
turned that down flat. I certainly wouldn't want to do anything
to distort the memory America holds of that great American. I'll
just be my plain self, and, in that way, nobody will suffer except
me and the audience.

THE LOVE LIFE OF SPIDERS

XXIII

How To Meet A Stranger For The Second Time

Last week in Montgomery, I heard a fellow call my name and turned to see a fellow greeting me like his long-lost brother. He was real glad to see me, the way he acted, and I figured maybe it was some guy I owed some money to, but for the life of me I couldn't place his face. But, brother, I want you to know we had a brilliant conversation for about ten minutes. I didn't write it down, but it went something like this:

"Well," he asked, "how are you getting along?"

"Fine," I said, "although I'm a little older than I was when

79

I saw you last." I thought maybe he would say when he saw me last, but he didn't.

"And how are the children?" he inquired. Right there I just about decided maybe he didn't know me either, but since he had called me by my name I went ahead with the conversation.

"Oh, the children!" I said. "They're fine." Naturally, I was speaking of children in general, who do seem like they're stronger and healthier than they used to be.

"Is Nan up with you?" he asked next.

That must be my wife, I thought, and I just couldn't stand to see the fellow embarrassed so I told him that Nan didn't come. That wasn't telling a lie, either, because Nan just darn sure wasn't with me.

Now it was my turn to ask some questions, hoping maybe I could get some inkling about his name.

"Where are you living now?" I asked.

"Same old place," he answered. "Guess I'll live and die there." As a matter of fact, I was beginning to wish he hadn't left there in the first place—wherever it was.

"What kind of business are you in now?" I asked. That generally gets a pretty good clue when you're in a fog about somebody's identity.

"Same old business," he said. "In fact, it's about the only business I know anything about." There were a lot of other things he didn't know anything about, like to whom he was talking.

Then he came up with a good one. "Have you *seen* Larry and Jane lately?" he wanted to know.

HOW NOT TO WORRY ABOUT

"I don't know when I have seen Larry and Jane," I said. I used to know a fellow named Larry in Mobile and a woman in Birmingham named Jane, who didn't know each other, and I actually haven't seen either of 'em lately, so I still wasn't lying to him.

"Boy, we used to have some good times together. Remember?" he asked.

"Man, do I remember! People nowadays don't have fun like they used to," I responded. They don't either. Folks my age, that is.

He was getting me into pretty close quarters about then, so I decided I had better get on the defensive again. "How is your wife?" I inquired.

"Which one?" he asked, very seriously. "Well," I stammered, "either one." Actually it didn't make any difference which one he told me about as I didn't know one from the other.

"You know, my first wife and I got a divorce," he explained, "and I got married again. However, my second wife got a divorce and now I've started going with my first wife again. That's why I asked which one you were asking about."

Things were getting too complicated for me, so I started saying how I had to meet a fellow in a few minutes and how much I enjoyed seeing him again, with emphasis on that "again." He suggested that I give him a ring should I ever pass through his town. Said his name was in the directory. All I don't know about him is his name and in what town to look up his phone number.

The idea of another get-together kind of appeals to me, in a way, though. We might find out who in the heck we are.

XXIV

Caruso Needed Sideburns

In Tupelo, Mississippi, they have started a fund drive to raise a half-million dollars to complete the Elvis Presley Municipal Park, which is located adjacent to the well-known singer's birthplace. The Mayor of the town hopes to have the park completed by the time Elvis is released from the Army early in 1960.

Well sir, that does it! There just isn't any use fighting this rock and roll business any longer. For fifty years I've tried to save my money and amount to something in life. The fact that I didn't succeed in either effort is beside the point. A person is supposed to get some credit for just trying, but right now the prospects of having a park named in my honor are mighty remote.

HOW NOT TO WORRY ABOUT

When I read about that park business and how they're honoring Elvis, I got to thinking about a very wonderful lady who taught music here for nigh on to 30 years. She labored long and late with untalented pupils, trying to teach 'em enough so they could stagger through a piano rendition of The Crippled Butterfly on commencement night. She tried to instill in her pupils understanding and appreciation of great music. When, on mighty few occasions, a student rewarded her with an outstanding performance, she beamed with pleasure and figured maybe her work was not in vain. I reckon, too, she shed a few tears for those who fell by the wayside. She did accomplish a lot in the years she labored so patiently and hundreds of men and women owe their love of good music to this fine woman. Nobody ever named a park in her honor and nobody ever will. There is a park, though, named for Elvis Presley.

Elvis accumulated a guitar in Mississippi, a hound dog and sideburns in Tennessee and a healthy bank account in Hollywood. For several years he kept up the government and I reckon they figured they owed him something, so they put him in the Army and are feeding him for a year or so. Actually, I think the Government goofed on Elvis. His income would have bought a new tank every month, but lots of people felt he should, like all other young men, do his part for the defense of his country. Personally speaking, I don't feel any safer at night with him in the Army. In a real crowded battle he might be able to knock out a few enemy soldiers swinging his hips around and he might be able to bash a few in the head with his guitar, but I had far rather see him back as a civilian helping me finance the government. His induction sure did put a load on me.

Some of Elvis' admirers are sure to write me hot letters saying I'm just jealous of his success, and they will be so right! I want his fans to know, though, that I'm with 'em from here on out. If a fellow can get a park named for him before he's 25, he should be President by the time he's 40, and if this rock and roll music spreads over the globe like it has here in this country, he might even get elected World Boss some of these days.

You people shouldn't be too hard on rock and roll music and us Elvis Presley fans. Mighty few people would turn their backs on fame and fortune. For the millions Elvis has made I not only would sing about a hound dog—I'd sleep with one.

Here in our town of 2,425 people we have an outstanding Mayor who does not have a park named in his honor. We have a capable bank president, some fine lawyers and some highly successful merchants, all of whom have contributed much to the growth and prosperity of our town, but none of 'em have a park named after them. The trouble is they can't play a guitar.

It looks like, the way things are going, parents had better buy their children a guitar and teach 'em to drive a Cadillac.

Which Way Is The Female Order Houses?

If you ever buy anything from a mail-order house—especially something foolish—they swap your name aound and pretty soon you are flooded with "attractive offers." Years ago I got a postal card from some firm in Chicago offering an "amazing" bargain in high-powered binoculars. I ordered the things and I imagine the company made more money out of selling other firms my name than they did out of the $12.98 binoculars.

A few weeks ago a record company offered me 12 long-playing records with short parts from all the great classical tunes. They were so long-haired I couldn't pronounce the names of half of 'em. I didn't fall for that particular offer, figuring I could get by with "Sugar in the Morning" without it costing me anything.

This week I got a card that topped 'em all. It is now possible, the card said, for me to get a hand-colored Coat of Arms of the Tucker family. It is beautifully executed in water colors—on a fine, heavy antique paper measuring 8 x 12 inches—and is complete with shield, helmet, mantling and crest, with the name in Old English placed below the bearing. The heraldic description is included with each painting and they also include a bibliography for tracing particular family lines. All work, they say, is based upon careful research. For ten bucks I can get all that information, plus the Coat of Arms.

After I got that card, I set out to make a list of things I either wanted or needed. The list started off with a new automobile and wound up with a wiggle-worm bed and nowhere among the foolish things I put down in between did I mention a Coat of Arms. I reckon I can get by without one of those things as well as anybody in the whole United States. I can get by powerfully well, too, without tracing my ancestors. I like to think of 'em maybe as good, conscientious and friendly people, but if I started out to track 'em down, I would probably find that half of 'em wound up in Texas after stealing a horse. Lots of those who stole a horse and didn't make it to Texas probably died of a tight feeling around the neck, commonly called rope-itis.

These Coats of arms are pretty silly looking things, anyway. Most of 'em I've seen have a spear, a shield, a sword, a horse with wings and a rampant lion stuck on 'em some place. If the Tucker Coat of Arms has a rampant lion on it I sure would send it back in a hurry, because us Tuckers have always been scared as heck of lions. Especially rampant lions.

To start with, you never know whether stuff like that is authentic or not. If I should order one, which I'm not, and they sent me one, which they aren't, with a picture of a fishing pole, a hound dog and a fat 'coon on it, I sure would keep it and I'd figure those folks were personally acquainted with my ancestors. A shade tree and a hammock down in the right-hand corner would make it look even more authentic.

Lots of times we're better off not knowing too much about our ancestors. When I was very young one of my uncles said that one of my grandfathers was once Governor of South Carolina or maybe North Carolina, I don't remember which. For a long time I was right proud of having a Governor in my family, but here lately I never mention it, and if anybody else mentions it, I tell 'em there wasn't nothing to it and point out how easy it is for malicious lies like that to get started.

Most of the ancestors of the people of the South were run out of England for either not paying their bills or for joining the wrong church, and they left in such a hurry they didn't take time to pick up their Coats of Arms. I'm not going to send over there now and get something they didn't think enough of to bring with 'em. I'm still just a little curious about what ours looks like, though, and if any of you Tuckers ever buy one, I sure would like to take a peep at it. I'll bet four dollars it never had no lion on it, though.

XXVI

How To Give A Permanent Wave To A Bald Head.

A fashion writer wrote a piece in the papers the other day about how the women would be wearing wigs by this oncoming Autumn. Said she, "By Autumn a woman who is brazen enough to appear in a home-grown coiffure will be as dead to a sense of modesty as a girl in a bikini bathing suit at a river baptizing."

However, nothing ever turns out to be as bad as we often fear, and maybe this wig business will work out for the good. The more you think about it the more advantages you can see in it. For instance, you won't have to look at your wife when she comes back from the beauty parlor looking like a mechanical robot around the head. If a husband takes a sudden fancy for a red-head, maybe she can cool him down by getting a nice, new red wig.

According to this article, most women will own several of the things so they can have a spare while one is being aired or dry-cleaned. They will sell to start with for $25 to $250, but later on you can probably pick 'em up in the super-market for as little as $4.95 and get green stamps with each purchase. The article didn't say, but I reckon the wigs would do away with wave lotions, etc., which would certainly be the death blow to television. On the other hand—and this is a dreadful thought—the women might could give their wigs a wave, making their husbands put the things on while they did all the waving and lotion applying.

At any rate, it's going to cause a lot of confusion. A boy will ask a brunette for a date and pick up a purple-top. A perfectly innocent married man will be seen one night with a Spanish-looking brunette and the next night with a strawberry blonde. He'll lean over to kiss his wife goodnight and either feel a bald head or get blessed out for knocking her wig off.

Women look pretty enough as they are, and what I can't understand is why the bossy fashion people in Paris don't issue some kind of decree that would require bald-headed men to wear wigs. I sure could go for something like that. I have a few friends who wear wigs, I think, but they act like they're scared to death all the time. They have to take off their hats real careful like, and they're always smoothing their hair down to see if it's in the right place. If wig-wearing for bald-headed men could become popular, a fellow wouldn't have to worry all the time for fear it would fall in his soup or get caught in an electric fan. In fact, my head is already smooth enough, so I wouldn't have to go to the trouble of having it shaved and I could pick out a wig that would match my peculair type of beauty. Right now I kind of lean to the scarlet-red type of hair, on account of I've never seen a red-headed fellow lose a fistfight. Why, I don't know, except they can get madder than other kinds of people.

This new purple hair is mighty pretty and I might have one of them as a "spare." Long, purple curls on top of my head sure would make me outstanding looking. In fact, I imagine it would be so outstanding that people might not even notice whether I had my pants on or not.

After a fellow gets my age, he likes to relax and rest. Just think how nice it would be, in a few years, to take out my teeth, remove my hearing aid, put my glasses on the dresser, kick off my arch supports and throw my wig in a corner- That's resting, man.

Should Foreclosure Notices Be On The Front Page?

I always say that the most interesting news items are found over in the back pages of a newspaper. The front page, as a rule, is reserved for such things as murders, suicides, graft and corruption, statements by politicians and super-duper tragedies.

Here are some of the interesting things I read on the inside pages of my paper yesterday:

1. A woman had her dead husband's body cremated, took the ashes to a local saloon often frequented by her deceased

mate, and dumped the ashes on a table where his former cronies were imbibing. "You wanted him with you all the time," she said, "so here's what's left of him."

2. Mrs. Eleanor Roosevelt is experimenting with garlic balls, covered with chocolate, which she takes every morning in the hope that they will improve her memory. They are being recommended by a New York neurologist. Garlic, they claim, affects the heart and increases the circulation to the brain.

3. From rocket fuel they have discovered a new "energizer" which has the opposite effect of tranquilizer pills. The new drug is called JB-516 and is supposed to make people work longer hours without getting run down.

To me, this type of reading excels by far such things as stories about Formosa, Quemoy, Lebanon, Jordan, Iraq and Little Rock. In fact, I can just picture that woman walking in the saloon and dumping a jar full of ashes right in front of a bunch of drunks. I've personally seen women walk in a drinking establishment and grab a husband by the ear and drag him home. I've seen women bless out a bunch of drinkers on account of she thought they got her husband drunk, and in both cases it was most embarrassing, but it must be powerfully disconcerting to have somebody scatter an urn full of the ashes of deadfolks in your beer. It would just about drive me to lemonade.

This garlic business, I believe, will help everybody's memory. If a garlic-eating acquaintance happened to remember my name and where I'm from, I would all of sudden remember I had to meet a bus or something. Sometimes I think people attach too much significance to remembering things. I watch those quiz experts on the television shows and they can remember who was the last man to strike out in the 1906 World Series, the name of the pitcher and what the fans called the umpire who called the last pitch a strike. They can remember what rivers run through Lower Mongolia and the name of King James' favorite first cousin. I'll bet you four dollars, though, they can't remember to pick up a loaf of bread on the way home.

In a way, I wish I hadn't read that article about the energizer drugs, on account of I think everybody was doing real well with the tranquilizer pills. It seems like people had kind of calmed down a little and there wasn't as much scurrying-around. When people hinted maybe I was lazy, I told 'em the doctor had me taking those easy-going tablets. What I'm scared of is that I might accidently take one of the energizers. If I did I might find that I like to work. After all, a fellow who never has tried a thing like that never knows, and it could turn out that I would simply wear myself out working. That is certainly a terrible thought.

So, I urge my readers to scan the inside pages and dodge the front page. Through me you have already learned a lot of things in just one short column. For instance, you have learned that Mrs. Roosevelt, who has so much to forget, is still trying to remember. You have learned that it is far better to take tranquilizer pills than it is to get in the habit of taking energizer pills. You have learned that it is most unwise to drink with alcoholics who have mean wives. Somebody is liable to throw a dusty corpse in your face.

On this pleasant note I will close.

Hark -- I Heareth Thee

Words have always fascinated me and every now and then I pick a nice long one out of my dictionary and use it on some of my friends just to confuse 'em. I never bother to check on the proper pronunciation, which tends to confuse 'em even more.

One of my favorite writers must do the same thing. To understand his articles it is often necessary to have a dictionary and an encyclopedia handy. However, I just guess at what the big words mean and get a heap more pleasure out of them. Lots of times I figure he's in perfect agreement with something I believe in when actually he might be meaning something else. The way I do it often keeps me from having to write a letter to the editor.

It's odd, though, to see people looking around for big words when there are so many nice little words we never use. Take

HOW NOT TO WORRY ABOUT

the word "fetch." It is one of the oldest words in our language but you hardly ever hear anybody tell you to fetch 'em something. They tell you to go get something, to bring 'em something or to go after something. Fetch seems like such a nice, unused word.

There are lots of other little words I would like to use but I'm just downright scared of what people might think. Have you ever heard anybody say, "Hark!"? You may have read in a book where somebody said, "Hark," and you've heard it in the Christmas song where they start out admonishing us to be quiet because the Herald Angels are fixing to sing.

Little Orphan Annie uses it quite a bit in the funny papers. She tells her dog, Sandy, to Hark. Sandy is very good at Harking. In fact, most of the time he's already Harking when Annie tells him to. But, in all my life I have never heard anybody in my presence use the word at all. I have been told lots of times to shut my big mouth but nobody ever told me to Hark

Some of these days when I'm out in the woods deer hunting I think I'll stop all of a sudden and say, "Hark! I think I hear the dogs coming!" When and if I do I just hope they'll shoot the deer instead of me.

Maybe some of you might like to try this very splendid word out on some of your friends. The next time you have a house full of jabbering company and want to listen to your favorite television program just stand up and clap your hands and say, "Hark! Let's listen to the 'I Love Lucy' program." That Hark should certainly get their attention.

The next time your children are running all over the house killing Indians and yelling like all get-out, just calmly say, "Hark, children!" It won't stop 'em, but then nothing else will either. You might even try it on your mother-in-law. It's a word she has never heard used and it might slow her down for a moment. A very short moment, that is.

THE LOVE LIFE OF SPIDERS

Now that you have had this word brought to your attention, I hope you'll make use of it. In fact, I hope you'll Hark more. There's too much talking going on in this country and not enough Harking.

If Mary Had Lost A Little Goat, She Wouldn't Have Cared Where To Find It

In the papers last week were three little items that were very interesting. They were:

1. Husbands die before their time because the wives make them work too much around the house, says an expert who has made a study of this problem;

2. A scientist came out with a list of things that need inventing;

3. A United States Senator raised old Billy when he learned that goats were being used as rifle targets at an Army Medical Center to provide causalties for medical training.

Now, inasmuch as these three topics are not related and perhaps controversial, suppose we consider them separately.

1. This overworked husband business is probably the most controversial of all, so let's come back to it later on in this column. In the meantime, be thinking about it.

2. A lot of things sure do need inventing and a lot of things that have already been invented sure do need a lot of improving on. For instance, we need to take the noise out of a lot of gadgets. It took a long time for the automobile manufacturers to invent the self-starter, and once they got it invented they let it go at that, instead of trying to figure out a way to keep it from waking up everybody in the neighborhood. Car doors still slam with just as much racket as the 1910 models and a certain bathroom fixture sounds louder than Niagara Falls at 2 o'clock in the morning.

Naturally, this noise-reducing work will have to be done by an old scientist. The young ones don't care how much racket goes on.

3. If they're worrying in the United States Senate about what happens to goats they sure don't have much to do and might as well come on home. I'll bet that upset Senator never was around goats much or he sure wouldn't be trying to defend 'em. A goat is the only animal alive that doesn't give a mule an inferiority complex.

Our family had a couple of goats when we boys were very small, and consequently I'm pretty well informed on the goat

.question. A friend gave us a pair for pets and I reckon Papa didn't want to hurt the fellow's feelings by giving 'em back. They don't require much feeding because they'll eat anything. Just to get the record straight, though, they do not eat tin cans as is commonly thought. They try to, sure enough, but all they eat is the paper around the cans. Outside of that one misconception, though, it's pretty hard to tell a lie on a goat. They can and do climb trees and if you don t believe it I'll prove it by any well informed goat man.

Our goats got where they would climb through the windows of our home and this eventually led to their downfall. Papa had one of the first horn-type Victrolas in this section of the country and our neighbors would drop in often to listen to the few records we had. One of the favorites was "Uncle Josh at the County Fair." This Uncle Josh was the Bob Hope of 1910 and the neighbors would laugh and laugh at his carrying-on. In fact, some of the comedians still use some of the jokes Uncle Josh was using at the County Fair.

Well, one day the goats climbed through a window and one of 'em got up on the bureau and I'm telling you he throwed a stamping on that record. It was the last of Uncle Josh and the last of the goats. The next day we had a barbecue and invited all the neighbors. We couldn't play the funny record, but Papa had just got in a new one called, "The Battle of Santiago." It was a terrible thing, with guns and cannons shooting and dying men screaming and moaning and toward the end, when the battle was over and all was quiet on the Santiago front, they cut loose with the Star Spangled Banner. We beat the Santiagoans, whoever they were.

It all happened for the best, the record getting busted, because we would have probably been up to our beltlines in goats by now. The United States Senate has a lot to worry about, but the goat population certainly isn't one of 'em.

HOW NOT TO WORRY ABOUT

1. Now, getting back to number one, which is entirely different from goats and gadgets. I told you to be thinking it over, which I hope you have done and formed an opinion. That's what I think too.

XXX

Should Hundred-Year-Old People Call It Quits?

You'll hear people say, "I sure don't want to live to be a 100. Unless, of course, I can still be active and not be a burden on somebody." As for me, I want to live to be a 100 even if I'm not active and have to have somebody put my teeth in for me at mealtime and push me around the house in a wheelchair.

A man who has reached a hundred has seen a lot of changes. He's witnessed the passing of the buggy and the half-moon decorated building and seen the advent of the chromium-plated automobile and the pink bath-room fixtures. He has gone through the kerosene era, into the electric age and now stands on the threshold of the atomic era. If he has accomplished anything he has made ten thousand friends and twenty thousand enemies. However, he has certainly outlived a lot of enemies which is a powerfully good way to get rid of 'em. He has been through panics, depressions and recessions, good times and boom times. He has worked for as little as 50c a day and as much as $20. and the four-bits bought as many groceries as the twenty bucks.

It a person doesn't want to live to be a hundred, though, there are sure plenty of ways to head it off. He can take a couple of drinks and get out on the highway on a holiday week-end and keep not only himself but a lot of other people from becoming centenarians. Or, if you want to, you can work yourself to death while you're young and let your rich widow have a try at reaching a hundred.

Medical authorities say now that the time will come when the average life of man will be about a hundred years and maybe longer. Nearly every year now they're finding ways to effectively combat many of the main killers and pretty soon all they'll have left to work on will be common colds, hay fever and ordinary aches and pains.

Proceeding on the theory that I'm going to live to be a 100, I've been figuring what I'm going to tell the newspaper boys when they come around to get an interview. All of the others say they always took a little "toddy" every day, got plenty of exercise and fresh air and went to bed early and got up early. I'm going to attribute my longevity to laying off of English peas and spinach, resting throughout the day and staying in bed until a respectable hour in the morning. I figure a lot of people catch colds getting up early when there's a frost on the ground and, too, a fellow should kind of let the early morning traffic get out of the way before starting to work.

It sure would be a good joke on the government if people could start living to be a hundred. Like it is now a fellow pays social security taxes until he's 65, after which he dies and fails to collect very much. Just think of living off the government for 35 long years without even hitting a lick at a snake! Think what a good joke it would be if a young woman married a 65 year old man, thinking he would pass away after a short time, and then having to put up with him for 35 years! A criminal, just given a sentence of 99 years, could say to the Judge, "I'll sure fix you for this, the minute I get out."

I'm sure strong for this 100 year business. I've just figured out that a fellow, in a hundred years, could catch a million bream, two hundred thousand bass and no telling how many catfish.

You young sprouts of 65 had sure better see that your social security account is in proper shape.

XXXI

Should Mechanical Robots Vote Before They're 21?

A mechanical man created quite a furore in Washington last week. Named "Elektro" and weighing 260 pounds, it was displayed there by the builder, J. M. Barnett, of the Westinghouse company.

Elektro can walk, talk and play the piano. Just why the thing was sent to Washington is a puzzle to me. They just got rid of a man up there who could do all three of those things and do 'em better. Maybe the mechanical man can do 'em more economically, though.

THE LOVE LIFE OF SPIDERS

The metal monster can tell the difference in color and count up to ten. He has no brains, but that probably didn't cause much of a commotion in Washington, where they are accustomed to seeing Senators and Congressmen every day.

What I think created so much interest in the mechanical man was the fact that he just spoke right out and what he said was clear, concise and easy to understand. That was something new in Washington. No double-talk. The metal monster is going to be under a big handicap around the Nation's Capital. He can't claim he was misquoted or misunderstood.

Chewing bubble gum is another accomplishment of Mr. Barnett's monstrosity, according to a reporter who saw the demonstration. This is probably an indication there's a loose screw somewhere.

Elektro smokes but isn't able to drink coffee. He ain't got nothing on me. I'm not able to drink it either.

It must be nice to create such a man-like gadget, but what purpose will it serve? Of what value is it except to make men marvel and women gasp? What inventors had better be doing is trying to make things simpler instead of more complex.

For instance, did you ever have the water closet on a commode go kerflooey? And did you try to fix it yourself to save a plumber's bill? I have, and when I was through I was wringing wet and the bathroom was knee-deep in water. The mechanism doesn't look too complicated but I wind up ten years behind on my religion and finally have to either call in a plumber or buy a life preserver.

Television manufacturers warn you not to attempt to fix your set because you're liable to get bad shocked. Call a repair man and you're bound to get shocked.

We need simple gadgets that can be repaired by the owner if they go bad. They make can openers nowadays that require a degree in engineering to operate. Before making a mechanical man Mr. Barnett should have perfected the mechanical pencil. I have a drawer full of the things that appear to be in perfect condition, except they won't write. They might also invent a cigarette lighter that will work right after you brag about what a good one it is.

Another thing they might be working on is an automobile carburetor that's allergic to liquor fumes and an accelerator unresponsive to the touch of alcoholic toes.

You Don't Have To Be Smart To Have Parents

A lady who read a recent column of mine about the disadvantages of being a bachelor has suggested that I write a column about how to control children. She says most articles pertaining to such subjects are written by old maids and she would like to have the advice and suggestions of an old bachelor. Well, sir, I want her to know I can sure do it.

Obedience must be taught a child when they are infants. If they start crying at night, don't get out of bed and pick them up. This is what they want and it will only lead to more of the same thing each succeeding night. A child will generally cry for about two hours if left alone. Naturally, this interferes with the sleep of the parents and many of them weaken. The thing to do is get out of bed and go sleep in the car.

HOW NOT TO WORRY ABOUT

Many children, when they get about four years old, will cry and throw a fit in public when refused an ice cream cone or candy. Many parents, rather than be embarrassed by the tantrums of their children, will go ahead and let them have their way, buying them whatever they want rather than to have a scene. This is a mistake, but I certainly don't know what to advise. You can whip the child, then and there, which will merely prolong the fit, or you can go ahead and buy them the ice cream. After all, it's worth a dime not to have so much heck-raising.

After the children start to school and need to do their home work, it is often difficult to make them quit looking at television. What you do in this case is to simply tell them to turn off the set and start studying. If there are any questions, simply send us a stamped, addressed envelope for further details.

If your child doesn't make good grades, the blame, about one out of a hundred times, can be placed on the teacher. So, the thing to do is to go see the teacher and ask her why she doesn't like Johnny. Some of these days Johnny's teacher is going to lose her temper and tell Johnny's mother the truth about the little brat and I just hope I'm close enough to hear it.

The teen-age child presents a very difficult problem. Thirty year old parents are very old-fashioned, you know, and they don't want their children to have any fun. To hear your child tell it, Mary's mother lets her go to dances and stay out late at night and Junior's father lets him have the car, even though he doesn't have a driver's license. The thing to do here is to inform the child that you have more sense than Mary's and Junior's parents and that you simply aren't going to let them have their way and that's final. Of course, it isn't final, but sometimes you can put them off for a few months. Stress to the teen-ager the wonderful times you had when you were their age going on kodaking parties, box-suppers and church socials. You don't have to tell them about the dances and house parties you were in on.

Finally, though, the teen-ager will win out and you'll let him have the car. As soon as he leaves, take two sleeping pills, which are good for about four hours, and by the time you wake up maybe they'll be back with the car intact and no broken bones or cuts.

Then, in a few short, short years, you'll be worrying about your sons and daughters getting married. You might as well make up your mind right now that they can't possibly marry anybody as good as you think your children are, but if you want them to have a church wedding you had better act like you're simply crazy about their prospective mates. Otherwise thev'll get married before a J. P. in Mississippi.

I'm mighty sorry I can't give you any more helpful information on how to rear your children. There are, however, a number of splendid books on child psychology, which if used right, are very beneficial. 1. Get out book; 2. Place child across lap; 3. With right arm, wield book until child promises to do better.

Do Persons Need A Backbone To Have It Braced?

Last week I went to Montgomery to get my eyes examined, and the doctor gave me bi-focal glasses. These are the kind of glasses that cause people, the first week they wear them, to throw fits, break off relations with their best friends and commit suicide, in that order. If you look straight ahead you stumble over a box. If you look down you run into a light post. Take 'em off and you hit both.

My eyes weren't too bad, and I didn't just absoultely have to have glasses. I could have quit reading. After paying for the

THE LOVE LIFE OF SPIDERS

glasses I can't afford to buy anything to read anyway, so they don't help much.

Really, though, my new glasses make me look very distinguished and undoubtedly make me look much more intelligent. A street salesman has been trying to sell me a subscription to a well known farm magazine for the past two years, and when I passed him yesterday he didn't even stop me, I reckon on account of my new intelligent look. Fellow had a good proposition too. You get the magazine five years, a Webster (new edition) dictionary, a huge map with the State of Alabama on one side and the United States and her possessions on the other, an automatic pencil sharpener, an Ezy-Kan opener, a hardly-ever fail cigarette lighter and a pencil with your name beautifully embossed in gold all for the low price of 75c. Don't see how they do it.

Although I am delighted with my new glasses, I think I would leave them off if I had to go through with it again. Like it was I could tell from the headlines that the peace conference was failing, taxes were going up along with prices, and several men high in the government were suspected of graft. I still get the same news, only I always feel worse after reading the full story. I paid forty bucks to read about stuff that really ain't worth forty cents. However, every now and then you run across a bright and encouraging little item that makes you glad you can read. Last night I saw where a woman shot her husband with a .22 pistol from a distance of fifty feet and hit him in the heart five times. It makes me feel right good to know that enemy soldiers are going to have a rough time of it here in America, if and when they try an invasion.

When people get old, though, they might as well get reconciled to wearing glasses and lots of other things. A friend of mine wears everything they put out. He has false teeth, bi-focal glasses, a hearing aid, arch-supports and he says if they make any kind of back-bone brace to keep him from hurting in that region he's going to get one of them. The older I get the more I

113

believe that old people never quit suffering pain. Sometimes a new pain hurts so much that they forget about older aches and pains, and finally they just hurt all over worse than any place else. That's when they give 'em bi-focals.

So, when and if you see me coming down the street, it'll be highly appreciated if you'll kindly step aside and not let me walk over you. If I don't speak, think nothing of it. It's just that I don't see you. And, if you'll say something nice about how distinguished and intelligent I look, I'll appreciate it.

XXXIV

How Not To Worry About
The Love Life Of Spiders

The government puts out all kinds of little booklets on most any subject you can think of. Most of 'em are free for the asking. You can find out all about the love life of lizards, frogs and blackwidow spiders. You can learn how to build mole traps, beaver traps and lightning bug traps. Just anything most you want to know you can get a book about it.

There is one thing, though, that our government has shore slipped up on. They don't have any booklets telling old bachelors what to do when their friends bring little year-and-under babies in to be bragged on. I always feel so helpless and yet that bragg-ing-on has to be done or the first thing you know you'll have a couple of enemies for life. Through the years I have managed to pick up a few of the standard expressions and can do pretty well on some babies, but there are some that get me in a powerful strain because there just ain't much you can say for 'em. They don't have as much hair as I've got, which is just about none at all, and they're leaking at both corners of their mouth. Their eyes are shut and their fists are clinched, so you can't brag on what beautiful eyes or precious little hands they have. It's pretty bad.

Some of the babies, when they bring them in, are bawling and carrying on something awful, which I don't mind. It's the ones that come in cooing and acting so sweet that get me upset. Just the minute I tickle 'em lightly in the stomach and say some silly, ridiculous little something, they start raising unshirted thunder. Actually, I don't think it's my fault, but after all, they are doing mighty well before I started fooling with 'em.

Parents are pretty hard to please too when it comes to solicited bragging. You can't say much and if you get off to a good start they'll just stand there waiting to see what you're going to say next. I've found that it pays to start off slow like and wind up with a grand flourish. Don't ever get the idea that maybe you're overdoing the thing, because parents are mighty quick to agree with anything you can think of nice to say about their children.

The first thing you want to find out before you start baby-bragging is whether it's a boy or girl. Once I was trying to brag on a very fat, healthy looking baby and I said I'll bet that baby will be playing tackle for Auburn in about 20 years. I still think it was a nice thing to say, except that they don't use girl tackles at Auburn. Before you start popping off, find out whether it's a boy or girl. One way to find out is by asking the baby's name.

If the baby is brought in by just one of the parents it's a lot

116

easier. You can say the baby sure favors his papa or his mama, depending on which one has it. If they're both there, you have to be kind of careful. You say it has the papa's eye's and the mama's hair and if it starts bawling you say you wonder where it got that disposition. Most all little babies are bowlegged, but it's best not to get beyond the eyes, ears, hair and mouth.

I want the government to feel free to use this column as an authority on the subject until something better comes along. It might even become as popular as their book on Mating Habits of the Gryllus Negluctus, better known throughout this section as a cricket.

There's one little detail I came mighty near leaving out. You bachelors should never attempt to hold a little baby, even if they are thrust upon you. They might catch some kind of germ or something and you'll be blamed for it. Too, you never know when a baby is going to decide to—well they have a lot of new kind of safetyproof garments for infants now and all that, but still, you'd feel mighty silly and powerfully embarrassed if—well, if you should drop the baby.

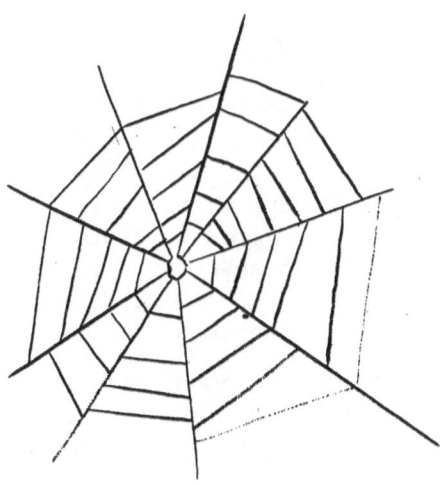

Does A College Degree Help You Catch Fish?

A graduating Senior boy asked me this week to help him plan his career. He was undecided as to what business or profession he should try to enter. Young people these days wait a mighty long time before making such an important decision. When I was only 5 years old I had mapped out my entire life, and I still think I would have made an excellent locomotive engineer. My Mother wanted me to enter the ministry, but by the time I had reached the age of 18 she was plumb satisfied to see me just as a member of the church.

We should be mighty careful when it comes to advising young people as to what they should try to become. There are so many misfits. Doctors, lawyers and teachers often find their work

THE LOVE LIFE OF SPIDERS

repulsive, but by that time it's too late for them to turn back.

Then there's the question: Should a young man get into some business where there is a lot of money to be made, or should he devote his time and energy to something that appeals to him more? They say that wealthy men find it difficult to sleep at night on account of worrying about their money. That I wouldn't know about, but I do know that it's powerfully annoying to stay awake at night trying to figure out where the next meal is coming from. Personally, if I had my choice, I would much prefer insomnia on a full stomach.

Looking at it from the outside, the life of a medical doctor looks pretty fascinating. They relieve pain, prolong life and have lots of new babies named after them. Still, I'm afraid I couldn't be a strictly honest doctor. If some rich and perfectly healthy woman thought something ailed her I'd tell her she sure was lucky that she came to me when she did and I'd nurse her imagined ailments along twice a week for the next ten years or at least until she got poor enough to get well.

Lots of people think a newspaper reporter leads a glamorous and exciting life. That's because those people have seen too many movies and TV stories where the reporter rushes in and yells, "Stop the presses!" Actually, 95% of a reporter's work is dull, boring and purely routine, involving interviews with filthy crooks, publicity-loving public officials, eager-to-get-ahead business executives and old women who want something done about something. However in spite of all that, there's something fascinating about it and if a reporter will work hard and save his money he might some day get to be the publisher, which is one of the serious drawbacks.

Some young men want to get in some line of work where they can travel and never be tied down in the same town. There are splendid opportunitines for travel in the armed services, but for constant moving from place to place, there's nothing like the college coaching profession. There are so many advantages in this

119

line of work. They are never tied down with a mortgage on a home and if they own a trailer they really have it made. If their team loses every Saturday they can get by a few years just by saying they're building character, but you'd be surprised how quickly old grads can get enough character building. It doesn't take any knowledge of football to be a head coach. All he has to do is be able to hire good assistants who can run the team while he's off talking to alumni and civic clubs.

The legal profession must be pretty good, but lawyers as a group are accused too much of lying. Actually, they don't lie. What they do is to get the witnesses so confused with legal terms that they do the lying for them. However, I wouldn't advise any young man to stay out of law on account of the lying angle. Most any business you get in is going to require a little lying and it must be nice to get paid for it. I've been doing it free for thirty years.

Unfortunately, most anything a young man gets in is going to require some work. If I had my life to go over, I would try to get a job as a game warden on some big hunting and fishing preserve owned by a decrepit millionaire.

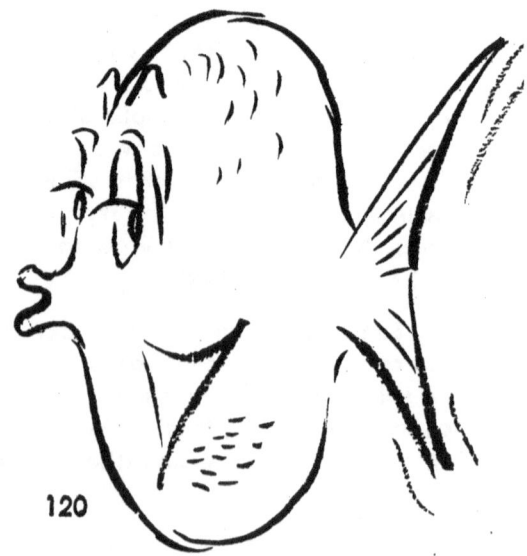

120

XXXVI

A Sleeping Beauty Is Liable To Pneumonia

A California state health official has started a campaign to keep people from staying in bed too much. The maintenance of a horizontal position, he claims, allows the accumulation of secretions in the lungs and this can encourage the onset of pneumonia. Legs idled by bed rest can develop blood clots, while muscles and joints often deteriorate.

Another thing, the Doctor claims, about lying in bed, is the demoralizing effects on the mind. He goes on to say, "The person loses the desire to get up, and even resents any efforts to extract him from his supine stupor. The end result can be a comatose, vegetable existance in which, like a useless but carefully tended plant, the patient lies permanently in tranquil torpidity."

Now that tranquil torpidity is something you had sure better watch. You might also keep a sharp eye peeled for that supine stupor and comatose stuff. Until they can find a vaccine for it I'm going to consult my physician if I have the slightest inkling that I'm coming down with it.

It just seems like a man, at my age, should be able to quit worrying about the various diseases. For forty years now I've devoted a good portion of my time just thinking what I would do if I should contract such terrible maladies as pellagra, cancer, tuberculosis and hydrophobia. About the time I discarded pellagra and hydrophobia, along comes this tranquil torpidity stuff and here I go again.

Right after reading the article by the California man, I read another article by a columnist who figured out how much of life we all miss by sleeping too much. Adults, he claims, need only 7 hours of sleep, which is two hours less than what I am accustomed to getting. It made mighty good sense, what he said, so I decided I'd try the plan. One morning I got up at 5 a.m. instead of the customary 7, and set out to town. If you people have never seen a sunrise, don't. It is a horrible looking thing. The sun come up all red-like and looks ten times larger than it does in the middle of the day. There is no noise attached to a sunrise, but the sun seems like it's going through all kinds of agony in an effort to get up above the horizon. For a fellow who has never seen one, it's real frightening.

Another thing, the people who get up at 5 a.m. are not worth talking with, and a fellow sure can't learn much. Most of 'em talk about work, which is a subject that never did interest me. What they do is to sit around a coffee shop until 8 o'clock and talk about what they're going to do that day. By the time they're ready to go to work they're plumb exhausted.

As a result of my reading, I figured out roughly that a person who gets up two hours earlier than usual each morning will, in 70 years, accumulate a grand total of 51,100 hours. If you like, you can figure out how many days that would be in a normal lifetime. I would figure it out but I'm too give out from getting up at 5 o'clock that one morning.

Maybe people should do what they enjoy most in life. If people like to get up at daylight and work in a garden that is what they should do. Personally, I never did like gardening on account of the notion I get that millions of bugs and insects are licking their chops in glee with each seed I drop. I don't like to get up early and have to worry for two extra hours about having to go to work. I don't find the air at 5 a.m. any more invigorating than I do at 7 a.m., and besides I don't want to get too invigorated, because a fellow at my age is liable to come down with a heart attack if he tries to do too much.

Anyway, I'll bet a person who dies of tranquil torpidity dies well rested.

A Small 960 Page Book On The Advantages Of Bachelorhood

Bachelors have to listen to proud fathers brag on their children. The fathers know that bachelors can't counter-attack and about all we can do is sit there and act like we're amazed that a little child can be so smart. You'd be surprised at some of the things little Junior comes up with and he's only 2½, going on 3. Actually, what Junior says seems downright silly, but years of practice have made me one of the town's best listeners-to-what-Junior-said bachelors. In fact, lots of times I ask the father about the recent observations of his genius son and you can be pretty sure he's said something. That Junior is going to make Einstein look like a retarded moron.

Grandfathers are worse than fathers. They brag about their grandchildren doing things they would have beat their own children nearly to death for doing. You should hear a grand-pappy bragging about his cute little grandson's throwing a brick-bat through a neighbor's window. Little things like that make them swell with pride and expound with fervor.

Most people feel sorry for bachelors. They picture them as lonesome, hungry, un-loved individuals with holes in their pockets and socks open at both ends. An independent survey, just completed, reveals that the percentage of bachelors with holes in their pockets was the same as among husbands. It also showed that it didn't matter much whether the married men had holes in their pockets or not.

Being a poor, ugly, uncouth, badly dressed bachelor isn't as bad as being a rich, handsome, immacutely attired bachelor because nobody is continuously trying to get you married off to some "attractive, young and rich widow." Being in the first category has, therefore, been a blessing to me and a lucky break · for the aforementioned widow.

Married men, in a way, are jealous of the free life of a bachelor. Wives detest them because they lure their husbands away on fishing trips, bind them and pour strong drink down their unwilling throats and bring them home late at night with thick tongues, bleary eyes and wobbly knees. The independent survey I was talking about also showed that more husbands get bachelors drunk than vice versa and there can be no doubt about the accuracy of the survey. I made it myself.

There are other disadvantages in being a bachelor. For 40 years now I've been sending presents to newlyweds, new babies, high school graduates, college graduates, silver and golden anniversary couples and never, in all that time, have I been on the receiving end of this giving business. Some of these days the bachelors of America are going to rise up and demand a plank in the platforms of both parties creating a special "Bachelors' Day" so we can get even.

In this article I have mentioned only the disadvantages of being a bachelor. If you are interested in the advantages, send 25c in coins or stamps for my beautifully illustrated 960-page booklet.

Would You Rather Die In Four Weeks, Or Wait A Month?

Several people have asked why I haven't written a column on the recently disclosed findings of a medical group that tend to link lung cancer with cigarette smoking. The reason I haven't written such a column is because I didn't want to.

All my life I have lived in fear of first one disease and then another. Looking way back I think the first one was "galloping consumption." It was simply tuberculosis without streptomycin. They didn't know much about treating it, but if you had money they sent you out West where you died in about a month. If you

127

were poor you stayed at home and died in about four weeks. In order to ward it off you were supposed to sleep with all the doors and windows open and, as a result, about as many people died of pneumonia as they did of consumption.

Another disease that people dreaded back then was pellagra. The doctors didn't know exactly what caused it, but because it was more prevalent in the South, they claimed it was caused from eating too much corn bread. Frankly, I think it was caused from not eating enough corn bread. Back then we didn't have viruses and vitamin deficiencies. All we had was germs and pellagra.

In time that scare passed on and people were cheerfully looking forward to dying with old age when along came the tooth-pulling craze. Anybody with a sore muscle or an ache or pain of any kind got the idea they should have all their teeth pulled and the dentists were most accommodating. In fact they pulled 'em faster than they could make new ones and I wouldn't be at all surprised if several thousand people didn't starve to death from eating nothing but baked sweet potatoes and cold grits while they were waiting for their new teeth. Actually, it was considered more or less stylish to have store-bought teeth, but the dentists finally put a stop to the craze themselves because it got to the point where nobody had any teeth to work on. They decided to start taking pictures to see if the teeth needed pulling or filling but they had to wait 20 years for another generation to come along before they could find anybody with a tooth to take a picture of.

We also went through the tonsil-taking-out period. If a 7-year old boy refused to eat his breakfast they had his tonsils out by dinnertime. While the doctor was performing the operation he also removed the adenoids, thus ruining the careers of thousands of hillbilly crooners.

People back then didn't seem to pay much attention to heart

disease, although lots of people died from acute indigestion and sun-strokes. Lock jaw was feared a lot but nobody around our neighborhood was ever known to have had it. We were continually expecting to come down with it, though, at any time. Hydrophobia was another thing that we were careful not to get exposed to. When I was very young there was a piece in the paper about a man who got mad-dog bit and how he didn't want to bite any of his family so he got a rope and went out in the woods and tied himself to a tree so all he could bite was the bark. It was a very touching story and I think most every family around our house kept a strong rope handy.

The fear of certain diseases goes on and on. Right now we are probably more conscious of polio, muscular something I can't spell and multiple something else I can't spell either.

So, after spending forty odd years worrying about pellagra, galloping consumption, bad tonsils, lock-jaw, hydrophobia and bad teeth I'm just about worried out. Somebody else can worry about lung cancer. Me, I'm going ahead and enjoy my smoking.

Why Not Red Undershirts?

Yesterday morning I came to town wearing a flaming red sport shirt and it caused quite a bit of comment, some of which I heard and some of which I wasn't able to hear but knew was going on. None of it was good.

I got the shirt as a gift and hesitated wearing it for several weeks, but I do think it's downright pretty. What I never could understand is where people got the idea that old people shouldn't wear gay-colored clothes. We're the ones who ought to be wearing 'em. Young people with happy hearts and bouncing steps would look good in black and white but it takes all kinds of color and loud-looking gadgets to make old folks look good. Actually, we don't look any better but a few eye-catching articles of apparel make people look at something besides you. For instance, yesterday nobody noticed my bald head.

There's no question but what clothes make a big difference in the appearance of a man. A real loud tie, especially a bow-tie, will keep people from noticing your double chin or greying hair. If you have a bay-window there's nothing like a pink shirt to divert attention from most anything or anybody. This article, however, is not intended to be an endorsement for pink shirts. Even a good idea can be carried too far.

Let's quit telling old people they should wear something "a little more conservative." If Grandma wants to wear a tight-fitting green and red sweater with "Hey There" written all across the front, let her wear it. And if Grandpa wants to dike out in a necktie with an Esquire calendar girl wiggling up and down on it, don't tell him he ought to be ashamed. Let him feel a little bit younger and a little bit spryer, which certainly ain't going to hurt nobody.

There are times when a fellow gets blue and discouraged and feels like maybe he doesn't have a friend in the whole wide world. Sometimes I get to feeling that way and I'll notice my shoes are scuffed-up and dull looking and the heels are run down on the sides. Maybe my socks show a few holes and my unpressed trousers stick out at the knees like I'm fixing to jump. My hair needs trimming around the edges and my old hat is flopping down on every side. All of this has brought on a form of the blues, technically known as "Neglectophobia."

It can be cured, though, thank goodness. I'll shine up my shoes, get new heels put on, dig around in a dresser drawer until I find a good pair of socks and then I'll press my pants until the crease sticks out like a Gillette blue blade. I'll get a hair trim and throw my hat away.

After I get all fixed up I'll put on my red shirt and walk down the street with my head high in the air and if people don't want to stop and chat with me all I can say is they're passing up a splendid opportunity to talk with a brilliant conversationalist and a highly respectable gentleman.

If a fellow knows he's as good as anybody, he might find

people who'll disagree with him but at least he's not going around arguing with himself about the matter. That's worth something.

XXXX

Scrambled Eggs

Maybe there is a kind of middle ground in this washing business. Some people do too much of it and some people sure don't do enough. As the great pop-off, Confucius, said, "When a man gets where he can smell himself everybody else has been smelling him for 3 days." Naturally, a man should wash often enough where his friends aren't thankful for a head cold every time he comes around, but on the other hand, he shouldn't be going around scratching his itch, either. When you get right down to it, I had about as soon smell a fellow as to watch him scratch.

———— 0 0 0 ————

There's just one thing that worries me about old people going back to college. I'm wondering how the motorists are going to react to a 75-year old man in a rat cap trying to catch a ride home. I'm mighty afraid they aren't going to pick him up, even if he has Auburn and Alabama stickers all over his handbag. I'm wondering, too, if Grandpa can stand the fraternity initiation and come through without a flock of broken bones.

Poor Grandpa, though, will probably have to pay his own way through college. He can't get a football scholarship, except maybe at Auburn, and I'm hoping the time will come when he can't even make the team there.

The motion picture industry realizes the importance of an appealing name. They see promise in a good-looking, shapely girl whose name is Bertha Brown. Well, I reckon they figure Bertha can't get very far with a simple, sweet name like that, so they change it to Beroncia Passanova, which gives the impression that she's from Egypt or someplace way off when all the time her father is a butcher in East Chicago trying to sell hamburger meat.

There was a man named Shakespeare who once said something about how a rose would smell as sweet even if you called it a pumpkin. If Shakespeare hadn't said it somebody else probably would have because it wasn't such an unusual observation. It does prove, though, that it doesn't make much difference about your name. I knew a fellow once who was named Archibalus Snodgrass and the last time I heard from him he was doing pretty well.

While trying to read a magazine in an airport recently a very talkative lady on the seat next to me practically forced me to join in a conversation. She asked me what kind of business I was in and I told her I published a little weekly newspaper. That's all she wanted out of me in the way of talk, and she took over. She had a grandson (this is his picture) and he wrote an article about birds for his high school thesis. I said I'll bet it was

134

THE LOVE LIFE OF SPIDERS

good and she said it certainly was good and the teacher said it was the best paper turned in and he got a 100 on it and I said what kind of birds did he write about and she said she would be glad to mail me the thesis when she got back to North Carolina and I could publish it in my paper and I said that sure was nice and I'm sure everybody would like to read about song birds and I certainly would publish which I am certainly not going to do, just between us.

———————— 0 0 0 ————————

All Associations look out for the women and see that they have a good time. They arrange such things as fashion shows and guided tours to places of interest. While the women are gone they have a floor show, staged by beautiful dancing girls who are trying to beat the summer heat by not wearing warm clothing. These girls do not charge anything for dancing. What they charge for is being patted and pinched by old, fat, bald-headed men.

Most all conventions follow the same pattern. One of these days I am going to slip my parsley in my coat pocket and, after I get off by myself, I'm going to see what it tastes like. Maybe I've been missing something. It was a long time before people would eat oysters.

HOW NOT TO WORRY ABOUT

XXXXI

With Toast

There was an old fellow who worked for us around the house years ago and he believed that the baying of a hound dog at night foretold a death and he always seemed a little disappointed the next day when he didn't hear about somebody dying. Actually, a hound dog barks at night for a number of reasons. He is either hungry, lonesome or has fleas.

—————— 0 0 0 ——————

After all, I don't know but what the best age to enter college is around 70. It seems like a waste of time to a high school graduate to keep right on studying when he can get out and make a better salary than the teacher who taught him. After he reaches the age of retirement there is nothing much to do and plenty of time for college. And, should he flunk out, there are generally no parents around to reprimand him.

THE LOVE LIFE OF SPIDERS

You can't tell these young people anything. They're tickled pink to get out of school and I'd be tickled pink to be back in it. A person of my age would give his left arm, his right leg and all his money if he could swap places with one of them. Tell one of 'em that, though, and they look at you like your bread ain't quite done. In fact, they think we're a pretty stupid lot anyway. I've got news for them: They're going to be just as stupid when they get a little older and try to tell the next generation how wrong they were. I would like to be so young I could listen to "All Shook Up" twenty times a day without having a running fit. That's young!

Young people, I think, fear old age too much, and some of our old people are to blame for it, including me. What we do is to take advantage of our old age. If somebody in a crowd has to get up to do something, we make a feeble effort at it, groanin' and moanin' and acting like we're down in the back, and finally some younger person can't stand to see us suffer so he gets up and does the job. We like to talk about how bad it is to get old, when most of the time we feel a lot better than we've felt in 20 years. That's on account of we're better rested.

A fellow, when he reaches the age of 50 or thereabouts, should start making a study of smart old people. That's what I did and I haven't done any hard work in goodness knows how long. I never get out to open a gate on a hunting trip. I never get around to actually paddling a boat on a fishing trip. Occasionally I do pick up an oar and sort of half-way offer to help out, but they generally tell me to put the oar down. Of course, now and then I do run into some mighty inconsiderate fishermen who don't tell me to put the paddle down. On occasions such as those, I have to develop a sudden "catch" in my back. There's

137

nothing like a catch in the back to get out of work.

——————— 0 0 0 ———————

A cow should be fed properly and given protection against the cold winds and rains of winter and the hot sun of mid-summer, but I doubt if hi-fi music with loving, kissing and caressing is going to make old Bossy back one of her hind legs and exert herself in the cause of extra production.

——————— 0 0 0 ———————

Lots of nighttime truck drivers have women in nearly every town and their trucks are equipped with loud-sounding air-horns. When they approach the city limits they let out with a signal of three longs and four shorts, which means, "If the old man is away, turn on your porch light." It worked pretty good here for a time, according to one truck driver, but finally some other women learned about the signal and it got where when he sounded his air-horn, the highway for two miles looked like Fifth Avenue on Christmas Eve night.

XXXXII

And Coffee

Last week I had a speaking engagement scheduled in Menasha, Wisconsin, the home of the Marathon Paper Corporation. The word got out and my friends started offering me various articles of clothing to wear on the trip to the cold country. One fellow gave me a heavy wool muffler and another loaned me a pair of galoshes he had used when in the army. Another loaned me a super-heavy overcoat and one offered to let me use his ear muffs but I turned him down. A Rebel ain't got no business going to Yankee land with his ears stopped up.

——————— o o o ———————

A mule is an animal that's mighty hard to like. They are completely devoid of any personality and you can go away and forget 'em mighty soon. They don't seem to have a soul, like a dog or a horse. I don't reckon there is a man in America who ever left the farm and worried any about what happened to the mule he left behind. Poets write pretty verses about horses and dogs and even cows, but I've never seen a poem about a mule. In fact, if somebody does write one, I'm not going to read it.

I heard about a wealthy Daytona Beach girl who dyes her dog to match the color of her automobile. Think I'll get me a Clarke County 'possum hound and fix him up with blue ears, pink tail and green feet and go for a stroll along the beach. The way they do things down there I'll bet I wouldn't even be noticed. Unless, of course, I had on long pants.

Thomasville is kind to strangers. We like to know what they're doing in town and try to help them with their problems. And we have a way of finding out where they're from and the nature of their business. If they leave their grits untouched on their plates, we know they're Yankees. If they're from California they're driving a Cadillac. If they come from the northwest section of the country we can tell by their brogue. If they're from Florida we can tell because they're wearing sun glasses and not much else. If they're from Texas they tell us. As to their business, we find out the easy way. We ask them. Our most difficult problem in this respect is when a group of women comes to town wearing hats. I'm just naturally scared of women with hats on. Every time one comes in my office it generally costs me money in one way or another. Have you ever heard of the "Homeless Dog Branch of the National Humane Society?" A lady representative with a hat calls by our office every year.

THE LOVE LIFE OF SPIDERS

——————— o o o ———————

Some of my resolutions, of course, I keep. The first of this year I said I would not eat spinach in 1957. I also gave up parsley. You see, most people go wrong on this resoluting business in that they put down on their quitting list just the things that give them pleasure. You've got to sprinkle in a few things to quit that you don't like anyway. Most anybody can give up spinach and parsley. Several years ago I vowed not to eat English peas and this resolution has worked remarkably well. Sometimes it's a little difficult to get the peas separated from the mashed potatoes but it can be done very adroitly.

Maybe you can resolve not to work too hard during the coming year. This was a resolution I made early in life and it has brought me untold comfort and joy. My many creditors have tried in vain to get me to break it, but I have showed remarkable will power.

——————— o o o ———————

Lots of you, after hearing the commencement speakers, think you'll be able to do something about the mess in Washington, brought on by the Democrats and the Republicans. I'm not attempting to discourage you, and I certainly want you to try, but you'll pretty quick learn that there ain't much you can do about it. The people seem to like for Washington to stay in a mess, and after a few years, you'll get where you enjoy it too.

——————— o o o ———————

With a bright New Year ahead everybody will soon be happy. We have twelve more months during which we can worry about a war with Russia, and as an added worrying attraction, we have the fear of a Republican depression. So long as we have something to worry about we'll be a happy people.

HOW NOT TO WORRY ABOUT

HOW NOT TO WORRY ABOUT

THE LOVE LIFE OF SPIDERS

www.ingramcontent.com/pod-product-compliance
Lightning Source LLC
Chambersburg PA
CBHW031129210626
46816CB00015B/1250